COUNTDOWN
The Second Jesse Sutherlin Mystery

"Eight years after *Copper Kettle* we drop in on Jesse Sutherlin and his wife, Serena, plagued by murders old and new beneath the advancing ⋯⋯ of the Great Depression. Plot, characters, voice all still at t⋯ ⋯rst book to this, his⋯

—Dana⋯ ⋯ak Series

"The cast⋯ ⋯a 'sweet mountain⋯ ⋯who can't resist lettir⋯ ⋯; because they make⋯ ⋯preciated series, but⋯ ⋯blips on readers' ra⋯

⋯d review)

"Unforge⋯ ⋯'s *Copper Kettle*, set⋯ ⋯mystery is fun, the r⋯ ⋯ith all its kindnesse⋯ ⋯Jesse and his astute⋯ ⋯017) will want to r⋯

⋯ers *Weekly*

D0448394

COPPER KETTLE
The First Jesse Sutherlin Mystery

"Set in 1920, Ramsay's satisfying prequel to his contemporary Ike Schwartz series provides fascinating details of a soldier's life during WWI. It's a genuine pleasure to read a story of detection that depends purely on observation and logical deduction to reach its conclusions."

—*Publishers Weekly*

"Set in the same locale as the author's popular Ike Schwartz series, but years earlier, the novel is colorfully written, with an engaging cast of characters and some pretty serious themes: death, poverty, and the strength required to persevere in the face of virtually insurmountable odds."

—David Pitt, *Booklist*

"…memorable for its powerful portrayal of the difficult lives of proud but poorly educated people too set in their ways to change."

—*Kirkus Reviews*

THE VULTURE
The Tenth Ike Schwartz Mystery

"Ike's 10th uses themes cut from current headlines to ramp up the excitement."

—Kirkus Reviews

"This is the tenth in this terrific police procedural series."

—Library Journal

DROWNING BARBIE
The Ninth Ike Schwartz Mystery

"This was one funny, great read. Starts off with a guy and his dog on a walk. The dog finds a body. A body that has been there for about a week in Picketsville, VA. Ike isn't in Picketsville. He and Ruth are in Las Vegas, Nevada. It's a little vacation from the death and destruction on Scone Island."

—Claudette Valliere

SCONE ISLAND
The Eighth Ike Schwartz Mystery

"Fast pacing, plot twists, and multiple points of view keep the pages turning in this consistently entertaining series."

—*Booklist*

"Ramsay's engaging eighth Ike Schwartz mystery takes the ex-CIA agent turned smalltown sheriff of Picketsville, Va., and his university president fiancée, Ruth Dennis, to Maine's Scone Island for a vacation ... Ruth and Ike's intellectual bickering will amuse literary and history buffs."

—*Publishers Weekly*

"The latest mystery-thriller for Ike provides all the fast-paced action and danger readers have come to expect."

—*Kirkus Reviews*

~~~~~~

ROGUE
The Seventh Ike Schwartz Mystery

"Ike Schwartz' outing combines high-tech detection with routine sleuthing to reach a surprising and satisfying conclusion."

—*Booklist*

EYE OF THE VIRGIN
The Sixth Ike Schwartz Mystery

"Sure-footed plotting and easy banter make Ramsay's sixth Sheriff Ike mystery...a brisk, entertaining read."

—Kirkus Reviews

"The sixth in this series has Ramsay's trademark folksy touch, a well-rounded cast of characters, and brisk and believable dialogue, this time with an international scope. Ike Schwartz's outings just keep getting better."

—Booklist

~~~~~~

CHOKER
The Fifth Ike Schwartz Mystery

"...A high-concept technothriller with a folksy touch and lots of local color, a winning combination that ought to delight Ramsay fans and win new ones."

—Booklist

"In the process of doing a favor for a friend, the sheriff of Picketsville, Va., stumbles over a terrorist plot...A fast-paced thriller that's quite a departure from Ramsay's Picketsville mysteries."

—Kirkus Reviews

STRANGER ROOM
The Fourth Ike Schwartz Mystery

"Ramsay skillfully weaves historical fact into his story, all the while blending brisk action with excellent characterization."

—Publishers Weekly

"All in all, this is an engaging enough small-town mystery with plenty of local ambiance."

—Booklist

~~~~~~

BUFFALO MOUNTAIN
The Third Ike Schwartz Mystery

"Ramsay demonstrates once again that he is a superb storyteller, adroitly mixing the spy and small-town mystery genres and shocking us with one walloping big surprise midway through the book."

—Booklist

SECRETS
The Second Ike Schwartz Mystery

"Schwartz proves as adept at navigating the philosophical/religious waters as he is at handling the more conventional aspects of crime solving. The result is both a thought-provoking examination of serious pastoral issues and a thoroughly entertaining mystery that succeeds on all levels without recourse to bombast or carnage."

—*Publishers Weekly*

~~~~~~~~~~~~~~~~~~~~~~~~~~~~~~~~~~~~~~~

ARTSCAPE
The First Ike Schwartz Mystery

"While Ike emerges as the most fully developed character, several secondary characters stand out as well, as Ramsay nicely mixes town and gown, sophisticates and rustics, thugs and masterminds. Ike Schwartz seems destined for a bright future."

—*Publishers Weekly*

Countdown

Countdown

A Jesse Sutherlin Mystery

Frederick Ramsay

Poisoned Pen Press

Josephine Community Libraries
Grants Pass, Oregon

First Edition 2018

10 9 8 7 6 5 4 3 2 1

Library of Congress Control Number: 2018936366

ISBN: 9781464210594   Trade Paperback
ISBN: 9781464210600   Ebook

Poisoned Pen Press
4014 N. Goldwater Blvd., #201
Scottsdale, AZ 85251
www.poisonedpenpress.com
info@poisonedpenpress.com

Printed in the United States of America

Acknowledgments

It is usual for the author to write this.

Sadly, Frederick Ramsay died before fully completing *Countdown*, so it falls to me, his editor, to find the words.

What a joy it has been to work with Fred from 2004 to 2017 on nineteen books: three Jerusalem Mysteries; The Botswana Mystery Trilogy, his brilliant standalone *Impulse*; ten Ike Schwartz Mysteries; *Copper Kettle*, a prequel to the Ike Schwartz series and the first Jesse Sutherlin Mystery; and *Countdown*, "the sequel to the prequel," as Fred and I liked to call it.

We at Poisoned Pen Press are immeasurably grateful to the Ramsay family, especially Fred's wife and partner, Susan; to Fred's vast network of colleagues; and to you his readers for your friendship, affection, and enthusiasm for Fred's work. It has been an amazing, delightful, always surprising journey, one too soon ended.

Countdown owes its final form to bestselling author Dana Stabenow, an ardent Ramsay fan, who stepped up to make it possible to publish this, his last book. Thank you, Dana.

—*Barbara Peters, Poisoned Pen Press*

Dedication

There is a story, told by family members, that in late 1929 my grandfather, J.B. Ramsay, was fired from his job as a stockbroker for Fenner & Beane because, they said, he and his kind were responsible for the Great Depression. Sensing the growing instability of the market, he urged his clients to sell short. An avalanche of people dumping shares created a domino effect of margin calls, runs on banks, and a resultant panic, which ended in Black Tuesday. At this remove, it seems unlikely that a handful of shares sold short in Spartanburg, South Carolina, could cause the panic of October 1929, but at the time, blame had to be assigned and the reason sixteen million shares were sold on a single Tuesday had to have a cause and effect. My grandfather's clients weathered the crash reasonably well. He did not.

J.B. Ramsay, like the protagonist in this book, migrated down out of the mountains and into "civilization." He watched the country pivot into the twentieth century and, with a dash of braggadocio and a fair amount of hard work, made something of himself. He prospered with a succession of entrepreneurial activities which included, if memory serves, a pie factory, a cotton brokerage, and the previously mentioned stockbrokering. I must confess, my only real contact with him was as a five-year-old (I think) and a dim memory of an old man seated in a wheelchair in front of his bedroom window, silhouetted by the fading evening light. And all I truly know about him I learned from the numerous and entertaining stories told me by my uncle, my father, and my aunts.

This book is dedicated to him.

—*Frederick Ramsay*

Chapter One

Smith's Ice Delivery Company, founded by Anson Smith shortly after the Civil War, had been providing ice in blocks to restaurants and residences for a little over sixty years. It prospered because its present owner, Willard Smith, had had the foresight to, first, add the distributorship of inexpensive wooden iceboxes to his business, and make them available to his customers on an easy monthly payment plan. And second, to invest in the machinery needed to produce "artificial ice," thereby eliminating the need to ship ice south from New England or the Great Lakes. The money, he'd told his contemporaries, was in the ice, not the boxes, which he sold at or near his cost.

You would have thought that a man with the acumen to realize the advantages of artificial ice would have taken the next logical step in the sale and distribution of refrigeration in its many forms. Representatives from both Frigidaire and Kelvinator electric refrigerators offered distributorships to him on at least three separate occasions. Willard declined them all. His cousin Marlow stepped in and, to Willard's great annoyance, now stood as his main competitor. With a dwindling market, Willard had been forced to centralize his business and assets. He decided he could redress his profit margin if he closed his auxiliary ice houses. These small distribution centers with their accompanying ice storage buildings and staff were spread around the county, and one by one he shut them down.

The latest one to be shuttered still had some usable blocks deep in the pit under sawdust. He sent Amos Krug over to collect them, close and lock the building, and bring the useable, that is to say, salable blocks to the main facility. Amos figured this job would be easy money. He felt certain Smith had no real idea how many blocks were salvageable and reckoned he could pull a half dozen out to haul downtown, then lock up the building and let nature take care of any still remaining.

At least that was the plan, until he discovered the body.

● ● ● ● ●

Jesse Sutherlin declared he was a "Man of the Century." By that, he meant that he was born in its first year and marked its passing with each birthday. As did most of his contemporaries, particularly those whose lives began (and perhaps ended) on Buffalo Mountain, he grappled with the changes in life over the twenty-eight years he'd spent on this Earth. At eighteen, he'd been to France and fought the Germans in the Great War, the War to End all Wars, and somehow survived. He'd seen the people, his people, on Buffalo Mountain struggle to join the twentieth century and had been pleased that they had made some small progress in that direction. Progress due mainly to the arrival of the Reverend Bob Childress. The cleric arrived fresh from seminary intent on taming the mountain. Some of that goal he accomplished with a call to Christian values and patience, the rest with his willingness to dole out some bare-knuckle theology. Mostly Jesse marveled at the rapid progress in society, from a life of kerosene lamps to electricity, from illiteracy and ignorance to a level of education he couldn't have dreamed possible eight years previously when, as a returning veteran of the war in France, he'd confronted his demons on the mountain and prevailed.

After eight years as a married man living on the mountain, he'd moved his family to Floyd. It wasn't that he'd grown unhappy with his life there or his house up on the slope of the Buffalo where the air was clear and sweet. Serena, his wife, had surveyed their situation, estimated their future, and declared there were to be no more bumpkins in the family. Floyd had schools that went clear to the twelfth grade. She wanted their children to be schooled, even if it meant giving up a way of life they'd both enjoyed and railed against. The children—Tommy, age seven; Jake, five and three quarters (the qualifier was important to him); Little Jess, age four; and Adeline, Jesse's daughter and the apple of his eye, aged three—weren't as enthusiastic about the move as their parents and whined that nobody had even asked them about going to school in Floyd. Jesse told them they didn't get a vote. The Nineteenth Amendment had done that for women nine years before, but it wasn't likely to be an amendment for children anytime soon. Besides, he said, they could always go back to the mountain house in the summer and weekends when the hunting would be good.

They'd moved into a cottage on the edge of town out Locust nearly to Hensley Road. They rented it from Nicholas Bradford the lawyer, who said when they were ready, he'd cut them a deal for its purchase. So, on this lazy Sunday afternoon, Jesse sat in the backyard on a bench of his own construction and admired the last of the Kentucky wisteria. Its panicles still kept their blue to lilac color even in late September, but the tips had traces of brown and there were nearly as many florets on the ground as remained on the stems. The first frost would end their artful display for the year.

He'd just opened the top button on his trousers out of respect for the fried chicken, mashed potatoes, and greens he'd had for his mid-day dinner. In a few minutes he'd collect the children and Serena, pile them into the Piedmont Touring car he'd bought off his boss at the sawmill, and head up the mountain for their weekly visit with his mother and a light supper, but right now, all he wanted to do was bask in the sun while it lasted.

Serena called him from the back door. He hitched up his galluses, re-buttoned his pants, and heaved himself up from the bench.

"Is it time to go already? Round up the kids."

"It's not that, Jess. There's men here needing to talk to you."

"Who?"

"They said they were police."

"Police?"

"That's what they said."

Sure enough, Sheriff David Privette stood in his parlor, hat in his hand and wearing a sorrowful expression. Since the sheriff generally appeared sad about something or another, Jesse did not concern himself overmuch about that.

"You wanted to see me, Sheriff?"

"Jesse, I am sorry to have to be the one to tell you this—"

"Something has happened to Ma?"

"No, I—"

"To my brother, Abel?"

"Jesse, listen. None of them folks has been hurt as far as I know. I came to tell you we found your father's body."

"You found it? You were in Norfolk and found his grave. That's mighty nice of you to tell me, but that don't need you making a special trip over to here for that."

"Not Norfolk. Your pa's body was found under the sawdust in Smith's West Oxford Street ice house."

"That there has got to be a mistake. My pa died from the Spanish flu in nineteen-eighteen in Norfolk, Virginia. Ma heard from a feller saying it were so."

"Can't speak to that, Jesse, but the body in the ice house has been positively identified as your pa."

"I don't understand."

"It looks like he ran into a thief. Not much to go on, if you follow me, but best guess is some jasper whacked him on the head and stole his stuff. Funny thing is, pardon, not humorous,

I mean, but he still had his money belt on and it had near to fifty dollars cash money and a letter from the Norfolk and Western Railway. That's how we knew it was him. Whoever did him in must not have known about the belt. Pretty smart, wearing a belt like that."

"What about the Onion?"

"The what?"

"Sorry. My dad carried his dad's watch, that'd be my grandpa, Ethan Sutherlin, his watch. It was really old and big and round-like. Granddaddy received it for thirty years' service in the AM and O Railroad which is now the Norfolk and Western. It was gold and big as an onion so, that's what we all got to calling it—the Onion. It had a gold chain, too, and his Jefferson Davis Guard medal stuck on it like a fob."

"Sorry, except for the money belt, the letter, and an address written on a scrap of paper, his pockets had been cleaned out."

"You're sure it was my pa? See, word was, he went to Norfolk to get work. He wanted to sign on with the N and W like his pa, my granddaddy. He reckoned he'd try his luck at the main office. The feller he was a-travelling with said he'd died there from the flu."

"Who was he, this travelling companion?"

"I can't rightly say. I was way off to France fighting the Germans. Abel might remember, or Ma, but she's been fading lately, so I don't ken how much she'll remember from back then."

"Maybe you'll go with me and help find out."

"I reckon I can do that. We were heading up the mountain anyway. You can follow us up the Buffalo."

Chapter Two

Jesse piloted his sedan along the twisting and rutted roads that wound up the west face of Buffalo Mountain. He could have moved along at a faster pace, but he had to consider the car behind him. Sheriff Privette had no experience with either the roads or the mountain and his Packard Estate car was not designed to navigate a road like this one. Also, lawmen, of whatever stripe, made it a practice to stay away from the Buffalo's coves and breaks. The folks who lived there were not welcoming to the arm, long or short, of the law. Some of that enmity was the result of the mountain's history of violence and its residents' independent streak which held that they could and would handle their affairs without the help of a people they did not understand or trust.

Then there was the problem created by the mountain's prime export: moonshine. Before Prohibition, the production of whiskey had been a cottage industry which supported the local economy in a small way, much as the gathering of chestnuts had earlier. The chestnut blight coupled with the enactment of the Volstead Act had catapulted this occasional avocation to full-time work for many of the mountain's residents. Whereas before, men caught with an active still could expect their source of extra livelihood to be destroyed and a six-month vacation in the local lock-up, with Prohibition it had blossomed into the nearest thing to big business. Attempts by law enforcement officials—Revenuers—had become more frequent and violent, and the jail sentences stiffer. Hence, the presence of any lawman, irrespective of his motive for being there, would be a major concern and subject to who-knew-what sort of reaction. If Jesse did not keep his guests close and provide what amounted to safe passage, a confrontation and possibly gunfire could be the outcome, there being no room for conversation once the intruders had been identified as police. So he'd insisted Privette drive the Packard, his personal vehicle, wear civilian clothes, and stay close.

Addie Sutherlin stood on the porch watching the caravan grind up the grade to the cabin. For Addie, time stood still. She lived in the same log cabin in which she'd been born. The logs had been sheathed with clapboards and some rooms added over the years. The privy had been rebuilt a time or two and moved when necessary. The century had turned, two wars fought, but for her, nothing of any import had changed. She still drew water with the pump over the tin-lined sink—as long as the cistern was filled. When the water table dropped too low and her spring dried up, water had to be pulled from the dug well in the backyard. In winter, when it sometimes froze solid, water could be a problem. That's why she made sure the cistern was full to the brim by early November. Lately, though, she'd become forgetful, and if one of her sons did not see to it, she might go a week having to make do with well water.

Jesse pulled up and unloaded his family. The children tumbled out and Serena led them to greet their grandmother. Jesse grinned as Serena moved across the patch of dried grass that served as a front yard with the children following in line, Tommy, tallest and oldest, first, decreasing in size to little Adeline, youngest and shortest, last. Like a mother duck with her ducklings.

"Son, you need a new hat. That one has had it. It is looking like one what we used to cut out ear holes and put on the mule."

"It's a very fine hat, Ma, and it ain't going to decorate no mule."

"Just someone who's mule-headed. Who is that with you that you brung up here to the house, Jesse?"

"Ma, this here is Mister David Privette. He has some news he needs to tell you."

"What news?"

"In a minute. Where's Abel at?"

"Your brother and Nancy and their young'uns be by presently. So, what news?"

"Let's all get settled in and wait for Abel. It concerns him, too."

"Land sakes, you is making a proper stew out of this visit, Jesse. Now, why don't you just get on up here with your friends and tell me what you have to tell me?"

Jesse waved to Privette and his deputy to alight and follow him to the house. The three men stomped up the steps to the porch and greeted Addie. She eyed them with the suspicion reserved for strangers in general, and flatlanders in particular.

"I didn't plan on no extras for supper, Jesse," she said as they stepped onto the porch.

"No problem there, Miz Sutherlin. Me and my, ah…friend can't stay. We just need to have a minute of your time, you and your sons' that is, and then we'll be off."

"Well, alright, but I ain't gonna feed you."

"Ma!"

"Well, ain't nobody said nothing about no company, Jesse, now did they? Well alright, then. I got some fresh-squeezed apple cider I can offer you and maybe an ice chip to cool it down."

"Well, Ma'am, that would be most welcome, and thank you. It's October, but there's still some heat left over from summer, that's for sure."

"Well, don't be just standing there, come on in. Jesse, you get them children an apple each out of the bowl on the table, you hear? Just one, now. I don't want them be spoiling their supper. Hey do, Serena. Any news?"

"Ma'am?"

"You still ain't got you a baby in the works?"

"No, Ma'am. Done having babies, thank you very much."

"Too bad. Children 'bout the onliest thing women can do that men can't what can make a difference in the world."

"I reckon four more Sutherlins is about all the world can handle just now."

"Maybe you're onto something there, Missy. Whoop, here comes Abel and Nancy and their two. So there be six Sutherlins fixing to turn the world on its ear, then."

Abel and his bride of three years trudged down the path toward them. When he spotted Privette, he stopped.

"It's all square, Abel," Jesse shouted. "Ain't no laws being broke or looked after here."

Abel studied Jesse's face, nodded, and continued his walk down the slope to the house.

"You'd better have a good reason to bring a lawman here, Jesse. Word gets out on the mountain and you'll be hearing from some folks."

"That there is about as nonsensical as it gets, brother. Listen, they're here about Pa, that's all."

"Pa? What about Pa?"

"Come on in and find out."

Serena held her sister-in-law by the arm and kept her from following Abel indoors. "Nancy, how 'bout you and me setting out here for a spell? Get them kids to running around and wearing themselves out so's they'll sleep tonight."

"Something's wrong? Is Ma in trouble? She won't tell them nothing, Serena. You know that."

"Won't tell them? What would she know that some outsider would want her to tell them?"

"Well, Lordy, Serena, you know. Where all the stills is at."

"Oh. Nancy, they ain't here about moonshine, except maybe to have a sip or two."

"What then?"

"They're here about Abel's pa."

"His pa? He's dead, ain't he? Died of the 'fluenza in eighteen, Abel said."

"Well, something has come up about that. Abel will tell you when he's done with talking to the sheriff."

Nancy sat back in her rocker with a frown on her face. Sometimes there were thoughts best left alone. The two women alternately rocked, interceded in their children's antics, and strained to hear what the voices in the house were saying.

Chapter Three

Addie rummaged around in her lone cupboard and found four matched tumblers. Jesse was impressed. He never knew they had four matching of anything. She poured cider into each glass, lifted the top of the ice box and with her ice pick, courtesy of Smith's Ice, chipped bits off the larger block and dropped them into the cider. Satisfied she'd done what was needed, she handed them around.

"Here you go," she said. She settled into the only remaining chair in the room. "Now what's all this news you be needing to tell me?"

David Privette sipped his cider, smacked his lips, and put the glass down on the table beside him. "Well now, that is mighty fine cider, Ma'am, yes, indeed. Now here's the thing I gotta tell you. We have found your late husband's body." Addie opened her mouth to say something, but the sheriff cut her off. "Now, 'fore you say anything, Miss Addie, I have to tell you he weren't found in Norfolk, Virginia, like you most likely suppose."

"Not?"

"No'm. Amos Krug was sent to one of Smith's extra ice houses to clean it up, you could say, and close it. Well, Ma'am, he found your husband under the sawdust out there. Doc says he's been lying there for onto ten years. In with the ice, that is, which is why he were in pretty good shape when we got to see him. Sorry, that weren't so discreet, but there it is."

"No, that can't be true. You made a mistake, Sheriff. My husband died of the Spanish flu in nineteen-eighteen in Norfolk. A man come here and told me so. I asked him how and so forth and that is what he said. Now you tell me, why would a fella make up a story like that? No, can't be. You got someone else's body back in your morgue."

Abel swiveled in his chair to face the sheriff square on. "That's right. I was here when we got the news. Ma says to him where and what, you know, and even asked about the money. See, he took all our savings, seventy-some dollars with him. The fella said the money was needed to bury him."

"And the Onion. He said he had to pawn the Onion, too," Addie added.

Privette pulled the money belt from his overcoat pocket and held it out to her. "Does this look familiar?"

"Why, bless me, that there is his money holder. Where'd you come by that?"

"It was intact and still on him under his vest when we found him. It still had fifty dollars, a piece of paper with an address on it, and a letter from the railroad. That's how we knew who he was. I got the money and the other stuff in the safe back at the office. It will be yours soon's it's been processed for evidence, if there is any."

"Fifty dollars? Well, imagine that."

"Ma, he must have kept twenty or so out for ready cash." Jesse said. "He'd have a need for train ticket money, eating money, and maybe rent for a room while he got settled in Norfolk. Looks like he never got there and whoever robbed him thought that was all he had. The Onion, though. Whoever took it either still has it or sold it along. Sheriff, we need to find out who's got it. That'll lead us to the killer."

"Jesse, it's been ten years. What are the chances we'll ever track the watch down?"

"Not good, I warrant, but it's all we have."

"Just to be clear, here, there ain't no 'we' in this investigation, Jesse. This here is police business and I'm putting you on notice that I don't want no civilian help. Understood?"

"Sheriff, you hop in this like a hen on a cricket, and I don't have no problem. But I am saying at the same time, I aim to nose around. If I find anything, you'll be the first to know. I'd like to think you'd do the same for me."

"Jesse—"

"Sheriff," Abel said, "it ain't like Jesse hasn't figured out crime before."

"I heard about that. Got my predecessor dumped at the next election, I'm happy to say. Dalton P. Franklin was a disgrace to the office. He wasn't even elected, he was appointed when Henry Spitz died of the flu. Well, he had a wife to support, which I suppose goes some way to explaining how the town council hands the badge to a man like him. And get that grin off your face, Jesse."

Jesse did his best but it wasn't easy remembering Bessie Sackmiller that was, nicknamed Bouncing Bessie when they were all kids together on the mountain. Could be she'd proved up on that nickname with one or two members of the town council, which would go a lot further in Jesse's mind to explaining Dalton P. Franklin with a badge, any badge.

"But the sheriff's office is rock solid these days. Jesse, you steer clear. You got that?"

"I hear you."

"Okay, then. Miz Sutherlin, thank you kindly for the cider. We'll be taking our leave now."

Jesse held up a hand. "You ain't going to ask any more about the man who said my pa was dead in Norfolk?"

"Like I said. He's long gone by now. It's been ten years. No point."

Addie sat up and fixed the sheriff with a look that had caused her sons to move quicker than a racehorse, back in the day. "He said his name was...something Smith."

"Smith, was it? Miz Sutherlin, do you have any idea how many Smiths is between here and Richmond? And do you reckon how many no good rascals will call themselves Smith when they're up to no good? No, there is no reason to pursue that end. No, sir."

"Sheriff, you can't be serious."

"Jesse, think a minute. After ten years, what Miz Addie is going to describe to me is someone who could be almost any of thirty percent of the man population in the county whose name may, or may not, be Smith. I'm guessing it ain't. Even if we stumbled on him, what's he going to tell us? He hears we're investigating a murder, he's going to develop a brain cramp quick as a wink. There ain't no future in plowing that acre."

"That's it?"

"Sorry, but got to be. We'll put out a flyer to see if we can trace that watch and fob. You stop by tomorrow and give me a description. Also we'll call in at the address we found on the paper. That's all we really have. Good afternoon to you all."

Privette and his deputy rose, said their good-byes and left.

"Well, I'll be jiggered," said Abel. 'Do you believe that man?"

"He's a good man, Abel, but I'm afraid not much of a police." Jesse sat down and stared at the floor for a moment. "Well, what he won't do, I reckon we will. Ma, tell me what you remember about this man who called himself Smith."

Addie rocked slowly back and forth, a deep crease formed between her eyes. Somewhere in the kaleidoscope of her memories was a picture of a man bringing her bad news, News about a dead husband, news that would be life-changing. How many people would forget something like that? She closed her eyes.

"He were a tallish man, weren't he, Abel?"

"Yes, Ma'am. Tall and dark. Thin hair, like."

Jesse leaned forward. "Hair color? Thinning how? Balding or just thin all over?"

"All over, Jesse, and black. Skin looked like he spent time outdoors, you know, burned brown. He had on a coat that had seen better days, for sure," Addie said. "But it looked like it might have cost a penny or two in the past. You know, like he once had him some money, but has fallen on hard times since. 'Course that wa'nt anything new since near everybody had the bad times before the war."

"Did it fit him tight, loose, or maybe it used to belong to someone else?"

"Well, that's a thought. Yessir, it is. You might have fell on something right there. Yes, the sleeves seemed a tad too long and the shirt he had on was maybe too big, lots of cuff sticking out over his hand, like. Yeah, I reckon he'd been scrounging clothes from castoffs."

"Or robbing clotheslines. Shoes?"

"Old and cracked and down at the heel."

"So, we know this about him. Back then, he lived on the edge. He'd carry a message for pocket change. I bet you fed him, too."

"Well, he did do us a favor. Well, no he didn't, but at the time…"

"Maybe Privette is right. The man could be anywhere by now. A fella like that can be found in any freight yard and trash pile in the country. Another hobo down on his luck'll do what he can to eat one more time."

Abel stomped his foot. "That ain't like you, Jesse. Lord, you can't just tuck and run."

"I ain't doing anything of the sort, Abel. Listen to me. Now, both of you, help me think this through. Abel, you were there. Ma, cudgel your brain. Was there anything, anything at all, besides being a down-in-the-dumps tramp, you can remember about the man?"

They sat in silence for what seemed an eternity. Then Abel's face lit up. "His eye."

Chapter Four

Jesse stopped in at the sheriff's office on his way to work at the sawmill. Monday morning meant catching up on orders that had been put in on Saturday late and some that would have come by wire on Sunday when the mill didn't operate. Still, talking to Sheriff Privette had to come first. The Man waved Jesse into his office.

"You're here to give me a description of the watch and chain?"

"That and more, yep. Abel remembered something about the man who told Ma about Pa being buried in Norfolk. It might help narrow down the choices a bit."

"Now, Jesse, I told you we weren't going down the road. It's a dead end, son."

"Sheriff, you told me not to interfere with your work and I said I wouldn't, but this new piece is important. It could help. See, it's one thing to track down a man who could be anybody calling himself Smith. It's a whole different side of bacon when you know you are looking to find that man that has a glass eye."

"This man was missing an eye? Which?"

"Abel reckons it were his left. And there is more. Ma says he had on what was once a mighty pricey, pretty wore-out old coat that didn't fit too good and a shirt, likewise."

"He was either a down-on-his-luck and out-of-work fella— plenty of them around back then—or he was a bum. I'm betting on bum."

"Probably you're right, but it don't matter. You got something to follow now."

"Come on, Jesse, this helpful bit you bring me is that I should look for a one-eyed hobo with bad-fitting clothes and you figure he's still hanging around in them same clothes just waiting for me ten years after he delivered a message up on the mountain? Jesse, ain't no way I'm wasting my time and my men belling after that rabbit. It ain't going to happen. Now, just tell me about the watch so's I can put it out on the wire and get on with doing my job."

Jesse studied the sheriff for a moment, sighed, and handed him a written description of the Onion, its chain, and fob. Sheriff Privette reminded him of some of the field officers he had to work his way around in the war. They were stubborn in their ignorance and too many good men were sent off to die because of it. He also knew that arguing with this particular version of stupid would be a waste of time. He waited as Privette read it through, asked a few questions, and then Jesse took his leave. Clearly, this policeman had no interest in, nor a willingness to solve, a ten-year-old murder. The chances he'd be successful were slim, and he had a reputation to maintain. An unsolved crime he'd tackled and come up short on wouldn't look good on his record come election day, but one he could dismiss as too old to figure wouldn't make a difference one way or the other. Oh, he would talk about it, but he'd not step out on it.

Jesse knew that he would soon be disobeying the sheriff's order to keep away. He did not relish the idea. It was one thing to throw yourself into a ruckus where there was an immediate threat to yourself, like in France in the war, another if the stakes were not high or so personal. Would his mother be better off knowing how her husband came to be killed and who killed him? Would he? Would anybody? In the war, he'd had to follow orders and do things he didn't want to do to people he didn't know and for whom he held no grudge. He didn't like it then, but he did it.

This time he had a choice. He could step back and let the story play out. He could say, "The police are on it. The sheriff will do what needs to be done." After all, nobody appointed him or even wanted him to play the role of an avenging angel. Yet, here he was, fixing to get himself mixed up in a ten-year-old murder. He pounded his fist lightly on the steering wheel. Like it or lump it, right or wrong, with the sheriff's blessing or not, Jesse knew that by sundown, he'd be at it. He'd go looking for the one-eyed hobo. If he didn't find him, he'd find someone who did remember him and, one by one, he'd work back the chain of acquaintances 'til he ended up on who he'd run the message for. Somewhere out there was someone who would remember the man and that would lead to whoever did the killing.

A decision made, he turned his attention to his immediate problems. The work at the mill needing to be done first and then to deal with the future of the mill. R.G. Anderson had owned it for near to twenty years and had prospered, but now his eyes and, well, his general health, were failing him. He'd made some noises about wanting to step down, but he had no family to turn the operation over to. Might he sell the mill? If he did, should Jesse make an offer? He'd managed to tuck away some cash in the last eight years, mostly by selling and buying timber rights on the mountain and the surrounding county. Those savings might make a decent down payment, but he'd need a loan to do the sale. He reckoned the bank would lend him anything he wanted. The bank was "loan happy" lately, what with the economy booming like it was. But he wanted something better for his family, and putting all his future in the mill would be risky. Suppose the boom turned into a bust? It had happened before and not that long ago. The war boom ended that way and lots of folks lost more'n their shirts. Did he want to take the risk?

• ● ● ● •

The mill hands were hard at it when he pulled into the lot and parked next to R.G.'s nearly new Cadillac. Henry Sturgis, the new shift foreman, waved him over as soon as he stepped out of his car. Henry was a stranger to the mountain. One winter two years earlier, he'd migrated south from up north like a bird. But he never flew back in the spring. He'd sought out Jesse after his family's business failed. Henry had, as he'd said, "shared a trench" with Jesse in the fall of eighteen. Henry had retired from active duty on the front when a German sharpshooter caught him peeking over the parapet one summer afternoon. His helmet kept him from being killed outright. The war was over before he healed up enough to rejoin the platoon.

He'd worked mills in the north, and Jesse put him to work. Henry spoke with an accent that the men he directed found fascinating and which they mocked behind his back. They asked Jesse if folks from up north all talked that way. Jesse said some. Others were even stranger. "You should hear them Maine people talk. Can't hardly understand them anymore'n the Fritzies." Henry, they learned, had been brought up in "Bastin, Massa-chew-sits."

"Yeah, Henry, what you got for me?"

"We are falling behind, Jesse. It isn't that the men aren't working full-go. It's the work is piling up quicker that they can tackle it. There is just so much they can do with the equipment they have to work with."

"Do we need to hire more men?"

"No, that's not what I'm saying. We have enough men for now. We need at least another saw setup, maybe two. If the orders for thin cuts for the veneer keep piling up, we could also use another eight-foot rig. We get them and then maybe we could pad out the worker force."

"I'll talk to R.G., but I ain't too sure he'll spring for that kind of money. He ain't what he used to be. Ten years ago he'd be all over this place. Did you know he wanted to join up? He fought in the Spanish war and didn't want to miss France. Now, though, he's sort of settled in like a broody hen. It ain't easy to move him off the nest, like in the old days. Like I said, eight, ten years ago he'd go over the top on a maybe. Not no more. Okay, I'll talk to him, but don't bet no money on it having any effect."

Chapter Five

R.G. Anderson had purchased the sawmill two decades previously and had turned what was deemed a shaky enterprise into success. The mill had fallen on hard times when the nearby hills and mountains had been stripped of their marketable timber. New growth of pine and cedar would take years to reach harvestable size. R.G. had been told by everyone whose advice he'd solicited, and others who offered it gratis, that he'd been a fool to buy a business that had no future. The price was right and he'd bought the mill anyway and turned it around. What his critics missed and he understood was that there was timber and there was timber. Softwoods used in the building trades was the traditional market they understood. They were ignorant of the about-to-boom furniture and paneling business. Furniture manufacturers in the North and South needed oak and maple, birch and chestnut for a demand that skyrocketed after the war.

The chestnut blight had devastated forests across the country. People were more than happy for R.G.'s crews to come and remove the leafless skeletons of once-mighty trees. Thus R.G. found his business provided with a nearly limitless supply of cheap wood which he brought in and cut to specification. By concentrating on processing hardwoods, he had turned a neat profit his first year and ever since. After three years, he purchased the equipment to cut thin sheets for veneers, paneling, and a new product builders were experimenting with: plywood. All in all, R.G. had himself a winner.

Then his health began to fail. His eyesight had never been good, and now, added to that, something deep inside was eating away at him. The doc said he'd need to make some tests but it didn't look good. R.G. reckoned he knew a thing or two and said not to bother. He'd rather die in painful ignorance than in painful knowledge. The doc said he didn't understand, shook his head, wrote a prescription for laudanum, and let him go.

Jesse found his boss hunched over his desk, a magnifying glass in his hand, squinting at a sheaf of papers. At one time, R.G. had the bulk and heft of his hero, Teddy Roosevelt. His friends would say he had Teddy down to everything but the teeth. When R.G. smiled, the illusion disappeared. Roosevelt's teeth, one wag was heard to say, were as "big as paving stones." Sadly, the comparison to the twenty-sixth president had deserted him. By now his illness had reduced him to a gaunt shell. The only remnants left of his Rooseveltian persona were his mustache and pince-nez.

"Jesse," he said when he entered the office, "I've been looking at these orders. We are way ahead of last year and it don't look like things are going to slow any. Can we do this?"

"R.G., how are you feeling? Maybe you should go home and rest. Me and the boys can get this done, for sure."

"Jesse, I know you can, and I thank you. See, here's the thing, I ain't likely to make it to Christmas. Well, maybe I won't drop that soon, but I for sure ain't gonna see Easter. What am I going to do?"

"Ain't you got a brother in Saint Louis? Couldn't he come and take it over?"

"I asked. He said he didn't know anything about sawmills and didn't want to learn. He said I should sell while it is worth something and spend my last days in a hammock on a beach somewhere drinking good-sipping whiskey."

"Well, that does sound like a good plan, R.G., but you ain't gonna die. You be too ornery. Everybody knows that."

"Well, that's nice of you to say, but bless me, it ain't even near to true. Jesse, you been making money helping me and I know you piled up some money buying and selling timber rights. I should know 'cause you sold near all of them to me. Whyn't you buy me out?"

"Well, the idea has crossed my mind. I might get enough together to put something toward it, but I'd need a loan from the bank. To do that, I'd have to know a bit more about the profits."

"Hell, Jesse, your wife is doing my books. Has been for near ten years, though I miss her not sitting in that front desk."

"She's got babies to tend. She works them books in the afternoon when they're at school or napping."

"Yeah, I know, but you tell her anytime she's ready to come back…no, that won't happen. I won't be here. Listen, you give it a thought or two. It's a good business and I'd give you a good price. Hell, most of the success we've had these last eight years is from what you did."

Jesse smiled. Well, maybe it was. "I'll think on it. Does the Cadillac go with it?"

"Well, sir, if that's what you'd need as a sweetener, maybe." R.G. stared out the window for a moment and then shook his head. "Broke his heart, you know that?"

"Pardon? Broke whose heart?"

"Wilson. He broke Teddy's heart. You know I rode with him clear to Kettle Hill."

"Yes, sir, I did. Rough Riders were a tough bunch. What about Wilson?"

"Teddy asked for an Army commission so he could go to France with you boys."

"I heard that."

"Wilson said he was acting like a big boy. He said nope. Teddy died right after that. The war wasn't over but four months and he died. I've never forgiven Wilson for that, no sir."

"Well, that is as may be, but I will tell you this, Wilson done

Teddy a big favor. The trenches weren't nothing like Cuba, R.G. There wasn't no glory and there wasn't no shining moment like storming up Kettle or San Juan Hill. It were a miserable life spent in mud and blood, and in the end, nothing got done. Black Jack said it 'bout the Armistice. He said if we don't lick these Heinies and good, don't push their sorry rear ends clear to Berlin, we'll just have to do it all over again in time."

"He said that?"

"Something like that, yes, sir, he did. I hope to heaven he was wrong. There ain't no future fighting wars and I don't cotton to the notion I'm raising my three boys for the Army to throw into a mess over there again."

"You have three boys?"

"R.G., 'course I do. You're the goddaddy to number one."

"Of course I am."

Jesse studied his boss and friend closely. Whatever was eating up his insides must have started in on his brain, too. What would he do when he couldn't get anything straight in his head? If someone wasn't there to help him, the mill and everything else he owned would either fall into ruin or he would be cheated out of it when it came time to sell. Maybe he should put in a bid for the mill, anyway, if for no other reason than to save R.G. from himself. What R.G. needed now was a good lawyer. He decided to put off any talk about buying new equipment for another day and also to have a chat with Nicholas Bradford about maybe representing R.G. That, of course, would need a sign-off from R.G. himself.

Chapter Six

Jesse stopped at Nicholas Bradford's office on his way home. Miss Primrose, his secretary, gatekeeper, and occasional destroyer of good humor, allowed as how the attorney would see him. She did not appear happy about it, but Bradford had made it clear that Jesse was to be granted access if and when. Jesse said he had a request and that it would take some time. He knew Bradford was tied up in a particularly contentious case and wouldn't burden him now, but Serena had baked a cake that day and if Bradford would stop by after dinner, perhaps he'd fancy a slice with a cup of coffee. Bradford had sampled Serena Sutherlin's baking in the past and allowed as how he would be more than happy to oblige.

Jesse drove home and parked. His next job: persuade Serena to bake a cake.

"Bake a cake? What are you thinking about, Jess? You think we got eggs and sugar to spare? We're doing fine, but it's pennies at a time."

"I know, I know, but I want to ask a favor of Bradford and thought he'd mellow up a mite. R.G. is slipping, you know, and I thought he needed someone to look out for him."

"'Course I know about that. I don't sit in that big old desk down at the mill anymore, but I still do his books here at the house. I see him near every week. I know he's ailing, sure."

"It's going bad, Serena. It seems like whatever he's got that's killing his body is now having a go at his brain. He's not making a whole lot of sense here lately. He's fixing to sell the mill and if he don't have someone looking after his interests, he'll get cheated. I aim to ask Bradford if he'll take on R.G. and be his agent, like."

"Why is that having anything to do with a cake that's going to cost us some money that might should be in the bank?"

"Maybe it's 'cause R.G. has been mighty good to us over the years, or 'cause Lawyer Bradford has helped us make some of that money over them same years. Or maybe it's just 'cause we both care about R.G. and also like Nicholas Bradford enough to whip him up a cake."

"We do? Land, the things you think up when you have too much time on your hands. Maybe you need to stay home a time or two and take care of four young'uns, cook and clean all day, and then have somebody who ain't got the sense of a bunny rabbit come busting in at the last minute and order up a cake."

"Thank you, Serena. I knew I could count on you. How 'bout I take them sprats off your hands for a hour or two so you can work undisturbed?"

"You are so thoughtful. Get out of my kitchen."

"I'll fetch some wood for the stove."

"You do that and then you get right back here and park yourself in that chair and tell me exactly what is going on besides you worrying about R.G."

"What makes you think there's anything else?"

"I know you, Jesse Sutherlin. I can read you like a book. Not a very good book, as stories go, if I do say so."

"Now looka here—"

"Wood for the stove, then we talk. Now git."

Jesse fetched in an armful of stove wood and loaded the stove. He stirred the coals and the dry oak flared up. In a half hour or less, the oven would be just right to bake a cake. If not, he'd add another knot. If it were too hot, he'd open the back vents and draw off some of the heat. Satisfied the fire was burning evenly, he sat and waited for his wife to speak.

"So, tell me plain, Jess, what's going on at the mill. All I see is numbers and unless I am dumb as a stump, R.G. is doing just fine. I am guessing that is because of you. I see enough of him to know he ain't hitting on all four, but he don't seem too bad. His mind is pretty sharp."

"That's just it. Like I said, whatever is eating at him, that cancer thing has started muddying up his thinking."

"How so?"

"He rambles. He goes on about this or that and 'fore you know it, he's off someplace else. He's fixing to sell the mill, like I said. He might could end up giving it away to some sharp dealer. He asked me if I wanted to buy it."

"You buy it? What did you say?"

"I said I'd think on it. Wait, 'fore you jump down my throat, I said that mostly to stall him."

"Mostly?"

"Well, it might be a good thing, if it were mine to run. You just said it yourself, the place is doing pretty good right now."

"He's making money, for sure, but I can tell this, he don't have much ready cash and he owes a bushel and a peck to a long line of creditors. If anybody buys that mill, they'd be all of a sudden owing that much again in debt. As long as the mill is operating like it is now, the new owner could carry it okay, but there's any fall-off in demand, if the bank called in a loan, that mill would crash in a minute. So, don't you be thinking about buying."

"Wait. He owes money?"

"He does. I don't know what he'd ask for the mill, but my guess is if he asked what it's worth without the debt, whoever buys it, will be paying double when the debt is thrown in."

"So, maybe letting someone think they stole it from him would be a smart thing for him to do."

"And maybe he ain't so befuddled as you think. Call in Little Jess. It's his turn to lick the bowl. What kind of icing will Lawyer Bradford want? His choice is white or white."

"I reckon he'd like white. R.G. is pulling a fast one, by damn. But do you think he'd do that to me? I thought he liked me."

"Oh, he does, but you know what he'd say…"

"Business is business." They said it at the same time.

• ● ● ● ● •

Nicholas Bradford complimented Serena on her cake. After a slight hesitation, he refused a second slice.

"Okay, Jesse," he said, "what was it you needed to talk to me about?"

Jesse thought a moment. His original plan had been to protect R.G. from himself. After his talk with Serena, that seemed less important. Still, R.G. might need help one way or the other, if not to protect him from shady buyers, from outright thieves.

"You know my boss, R.G. Anderson. Well, here's the thing I'm fretting over." Jesse laid out the whole situation including Serena's thoughts on the possibility that R.G. might be smarter than he let on.

"Let me be sure I got this straight. Anderson is selling his mill. You think he might be short in the brain department and because of that, some jasper might could cheat him. But you say that might be him trying to flim-flam the buyer into taking on a bushel of debt that he, that's R.G., would be shed of and he'd be the winner, after all. Is that about it? Also, R.G. is thinking you'd be the boy to buy the mill."

"Pretty much."

"And, Miss Serena, you do the books and you think that all in all, the mill is a big zero, money wise?"

"I do."

Bradford scratched his head and hitched himself around in his chair. "Well, this is how I see it. The way this economy is booming, the debt business will pretty much be swallowed up in the increased value of the mill over the next couple of years.

See, the way it's going now, shoot, the mill might double its value in two to three years. If it were me, I'd let him think he's having me and snap it up in a heartbeat."

Serena frowned. She wouldn't cross the lawyer, but Jesse knew she wasn't buying his line.

Bradford sat back and eyed the cake. "Well, maybe just a little piece. So, that's it?"

Jesse cut a slab and plopped it on the lawyer's plate. "Well, there's the one-eyed man I need to ask you about."

Chapter Seven

While Serena busied herself putting the children to bed, Jesse and Bradford moved out to the back porch. For October the weather was unseasonably mild. A jacket, or in Jesse's case, a hand-knitted cardigan, provided sufficient insulation. Sitting outdoors meant Bradford could smoke his Cuban cigar, a taste for which he'd developed over the last four years, but a habit Serena would not allow to be exercised in her house. The fact the house was Bradford's and she was his tenant made no difference to her. Jesse sat on the steps while Bradford settled on the wood box.

Jesse described the situation he'd inherited with the discovery of his father's body. Bradford asked a few questions, promised to ask around the legal community about a one-eyed bum, and added that Sheriff Privette probably had it right. After ten years, the chance a killer would be found was pretty slim and Jesse ought to accept that.

Jesse nodded. Bradford and the sheriff probably had a point. Sleuthing was something he'd done once before and he'd been successful primarily because he knew his people and could predict their behavior. This was a different kettle of stew, and he knew it. He wasn't on the mountain anymore. But this was personal and he would not and could not let it go.

Serena finished clearing away the dishes and putting the last of the children to bed and joined them. She hugged a woolen shawl closely around her shoulders and sat on a upended stump Jesse had not yet split into proper sized chunks for the stove.

"Lawyer Bradford says I should forget this murder business. He thinks Sheriff Privette has put his finger plumb on the truth of it. Ain't that right?"

Bradford knocked the ash from his cigar, pinched off the end and set it aside. He knew Serena's dislike for cigar odor, no matter how much the stogie cost. He'd finish it later. "That's about the size of it. I'm sorry to say that I don't see any outcome that'll satisfy you or the law, Jesse."

"I know you," Serena said. "You're about as likely to quit on this as you are to flap your arms and fly. Mister Bradford, you should know by now how mule-headed he can be."

"That I do. I reckon there won't be any point in reasoning with him on this one. So then, tell me more about the mill. Is it profitable on the day-to-day?"

"I told you it would be a money-eater. R.G. is carrying way too much debt to make it a good buy."

"Now, Miss Serena, I heard that part. What I want to know is about the cash flow. Can you pull enough to diversify? See, you know all about bookkeeping and all, I am sure, but business is another matter."

"You mean, past the adding and subtracting numbers, it isn't something a woman would understand?"

"Well, now that you put it that way. See, there are complexities involved in the world of finance that don't find a match-up with, say, running a house."

"You mean I pay cash money for eggs and you all pay with a line of credit when you dabble in egg futures?"

"Well, I'm not sure I'd put it quite like that. You're making a simple thing out of a complex thing. What exactly do you know about futures?"

"Next to nothing, for a fact, but I hear things at the bank. Folks going on about how they are deep into this or that kind of investment and how they aim to ride the boom into a bigger house and shiny new car. That's if the bank don't stop financing their gambling."

"It isn't a gamble, Serena, trust me. The market is strong. It reflects the country and what she stands for. Near everybody knows that. We are a strong country with a growing economy. You put your money to work and you can move up, too."

"I am one hundred percent satisfied right where I am at and with what I got, thank you very much."

"How about you, Jesse? Are you hunky-dory with your lot in life?"

"I ain't got no complaints at the moment. If you're asking would I like more, well, shoot, 'course I do. Everybody does, don't they?"

"Everybody 'cept Serena here."

"Don't mind me. I am just a woman not seeing the big picture."

"Like I said, you can have more, son. You get yourself into the stock market like most everybody else and play it right and big things can happen. Like the song says, you'll be sitting on top of the world. Don't you love Al Jolson? Anyway, think about it."

Serena gave a little chuckle and said, "I'm thinking it'll be more like you want to be a 'Big Butter and Egg Man' and then maybe the 'Turkey in the Straw.'"

Nicholas Bradford snorted. "Well, there you have it, Jesse. Serena here, is right, women just don't see the big picture. Now take me. I have made a me pretty nice little bundle by jumping on opportunities when they are presented to me. Was I right to invest in you back in twenty? There, you see? I know a good thing when I see it."

"Well, I reckon I can agree with that last part. How about that, Serena?"

"I'll give you that. But that's a man sizing up another man. It'll be about his character and such. How do you size up shares

in a company you don't know anything about past its price is
on the rise?"

"In this here case, that's all you need to know."

Serena stood. "Getting a mite chilly out here. I leave you two
big-time financiers to your dreaming. I have some socks to darn
and some buttons needing to be sewed on. Unless you have a
million dollars in your pocket you didn't say anything about,
Jesse, I'll see you later."

Bradford stood and pulled out his pocket watch. "Whooee,
lookit the time. I got me a big day tomorrow. Thank you for the
cake and coffee, Serena, Jesse. I'll be getting to home."

Bradford slipped around the side of the house. Jesse heard the
scratch of a match and reckoned the lawyer had lit his cigar. The
smell of burning Cuban tobacco a few seconds later confirmed it.

Serena was not darning or sewing when he reentered the
house. She had their bank book out and was studying its contents.

"Jess, I am your wife and you are the head of the house."

"But?"

"But please don't rush out and spend our money without
some heavy thinking. I know listening to Lawyer Bradford and
his plans can be tempting, but we are not that kind of people,
you know?"

"His kind of people?"

"We're mountain folk, Jess. We work the land, cut timber,
work with our hands. We understand that what we have is what
we worked hard for. Found money just isn't part of our world.
Mister Bradford come from another place. They make money
thinking about things. Writing and talking and maybe selling
some. The world for them is what a piece of bottom land is to
us. A good place to plant and sow, but for us it's seeds, for them
it's pieces of paper. I just am not sure we can move in this world.
It's not comfortable, you know? Not for me, it ain't."

"Maybe we can learn that world."

"Maybe, but not by throwing all our money into a sawmill."

Jesse nodded. She had a point. Mountain folk took some time to adjust to flatland ways. Some more than others.

Serena leaned against the kitchen door jamb. "You coming up to bed?"

"In a minute. I got me some thinking to do."

"You are wondering about the Onion."

Serena knew him better than he knew himself sometimes.

Chapter Eight

The sun had been up for three hours when Jesse arrived at the sawmill. Abel stood at the gate waiting.

"You finally going to take me up on offering you a job here?" Jesse said.

He'd been after his brother to sign on for years. Abel, however, had said repeatedly that he didn't want to give up mountain living. He spoke the words in a way that hinted that perhaps Jesse had betrayed his heritage somehow, had turned his back on his people, and thrown in with the flatlanders and all their evil ways. Jesse let the implication slide. He'd done his part, lived the life, made his mark and wished to move on. Since the war and the concurrent two years of influenza pandemic, he'd said, the world was a changed place. There were moments in time when the world pivoted and set off in a new direction. You either turned with it or you found yourself wandering off lost and alone. The old mountain and its culture had run out of time and place.

Jesse felt no allegiance to a way of life that kept its people poor and ignorant. Civilization would come to the mountain and, sooner or later, its folks would yield or die. Even now, younger men were drifting to the nearby cities and towns and some even farther to places like Baltimore and Pittsburgh. The mountain had played out. You couldn't farm the land, timber the hills, or harvest the forest. Only Prohibition and moonshine remained a source of income and that was no longer a winked-at-and-only-occasionally-interdicted pastime. It was a federal offense and, increasingly, revenue agents were raiding stills. That, in turn, had brought violence and occasional bloodshed back to the hills. Abel should not allow himself to get caught up in it, Jesse said. But there was no reasoning with his brother. He allowed that what Jesse said might be near to true, but Big Tom McAdoo still headed the family and, even though he might be old and not functioning too good anymore, he was the leader and his still and those of the uncles, cousins, and relatives of various denominations continued to provide an income beyond anything they could earn anywhere else. Besides, who would want to be beholden to some boss?

It appeared Abel still felt that way. "Nope, I ain't come to saw no wood for you, Jesse. Listen, I been thinking about Pa and who musta done him in."

"You got us a lead on the one-eyed man?"

"No, that ain't going to happen. He's in the wind, for a certain. But listen. Remember, this had to happen ten year ago, right? So, who would have been the likely person to come after any of us? It had to be—"

"Don't you even say them words, Abel. If you think about starting up that old 'us and them' talk, I will personally pop you one in the chops."

"Jesse, it had to be a LeBrun, and you know it."

"I don't know it, and neither do you. I ain't even going to think about it. We been down the road a time or two and I ain't about to go there again. You ought not, either."

"Well, you may not want to. I figured you'd say that, but I come down here to tell you I aim to have me a look-see. Just so you know and won't be surprised, especially when I come up with the who of it."

"Abel…Okay, I can't talk no sense into you. Mighta could once, but not no more. Just you walk soft and be careful. Things might have cooled a mite on the mountain, but there is still some mighty short fuses on both sides and it don't take much to set someone off. You better think twice before you go and point your finger at someone 'fore you have one hundred percent proof they done anything a-tall."

Jesse turned to go. He loved his brother and wanted more than anything in the world for him to come down off the mountain and find his way in this new world the big war had made. But Abel was stuck in a time long over and marching down a road that led nowhere, and Jesse could not get through to him. He could only hope the lights would come on someday before it was too late.

Henry Sturgis loitered by the office door.

"How-do, Henry, ain't you got something you're supposed to be doing 'bout now?"

"All under control. Say, is it true R.G. is thinking about selling the mill?"

"I reckon it's a maybe, for sure."

"You interested?"

"I'm considering it, yep. There is a few particulars that have me worried, though."

"So, you haven't made an offer?"

"What? An offer? Naw, too soon for that. See, there's the debt thing and—"

"Well, sure enough, nobody wants a big debt, but this mill is humming and, according to you, more orders are coming in all the time. Put some money into upgrading the machinery and such, and this could be a gold mine."

"Well, you might have got ahold of something there, Henry. Like I said, thinking about it some."

"Well, if I were you, I wouldn't waste too much time at that. Somebody will find out about it and whip that old carpet out from under your feet."

"Thank you, Henry. I'll keep that in mind."

So the word was out. Did R.G. plant that in hopes of drawing a buyer out of the woodpile? If Serena had it pegged right, R.G. might be up to dumping a heap of debt and getting out from under with a pretty nice payday. Or Henry could have got the good end of the stick and be onto something. Bradford had his opinion and it plumbed up with Henry's. So, what was Jesse, or maybe Serena, actually, missing?

He stepped into the office. R.G. was at his desk. Jesse couldn't be sure, but he could have sworn that before R.G.'s face took on its wore-out, sickly look, it had a bright-as-a-button expression on it. Now if that were true…

"Morning, R.G. You feeling better today?"

"Fair to middling, Jesse. There is a mess of paper on the desk that needs looking at. I just ain't got the gumption to handle it. Can you sort it out? I think we got us another batch of orders from the Southern Furniture Co. Ever since old Oscar Bolick switched from upholstering buggy seats and backs to furniture, he and us been making real money. And it's not just his Southern Furniture Company. North Carolina seems about to make itself the furniture capital of the whole U S of A. Anyway, he's asking for chestnut and cherry. Them others seem mostly set on oak."

More R.G. bamboozling? Jesse knew he should be careful, but there wasn't any doubt about the mill was doing itself a land office business. "This here about comes closest I ever seen to the Oklahoma Land Rush, only for good furniture wood, R.G."

"Business is good, Jesse. Money is there, if you know how to jump in on the moment, if you know what I mean."

Jess reckoned he did.

Chapter Nine

The economic boom notwithstanding, there were (and always will be, the politicians tell us) those who struggle and fail and must forage for a living on the fringes of society. Jesse's corner of Virginia was no exception. Transients had constructed a rough campground about a mile southwest of town. It did not have the sanction of the county, but as there were no close neighbors to complain, the police allowed as how they had real problems to handle and looked the other way. Besides, leaving it intact made their job a heap easier when they knew where the likely suspects of a break-in or a petty theft could be found.

While that might be an advantage, it remained largely untested, as most of the campground's inhabitants were just men looking for work, a meal, a leg up, a way out of the poverty into which their situations had plunged them. Women in the camp were rare, but not excluded. Once in a while, a man on the run from the law would drift in and then leave. Sometimes that was occasioned by an arrest, more often by the need to keep moving, and occasionally they just disappeared, their remains to be discovered months later and miles away.

Jesse strapped on his Army-issue Colt automatic and drove out to the camp. If there was anyone who might remember a one-eyed bum with ill-fitting clothes, he'd most likely be found in the camp. It was a long shot, but what else did he have? He parked on the side of the county road, a few hundred yards north of where he expected to find the camp, and set out through the woods. The trees effectively screened it from the road. The town clock had struck eight when he drove through. The men looking for work would be out and about. Those who'd given up hope would still be there plotting which farm to raid for a chicken, or smokehouse to filch a side of bacon, or they'd be waiting for word from the more enterprising of their number as to where they might cadge a meal.

Jesse paused at the edge of the site and lingered in the shadows of the pines and oaks. He narrowed his eyes and scanned the layout. Crude shacks built from lumber scraps, cardboard, and canvas were tucked in and among the trees. A few seemed to have been there for some time. Others might have been thrown together days or even hours ago. He didn't see any sign of a privy and realized, he hoped not too late, he'd need to watch his step. He saw a stirring in one tent-like structure and watched as a tall and very slender man emerged. He stretched, scratched, and shuffled off into the woods. Jesse decided he would wait until the man finished his business before he took him on. While he waited, Jesse inspected the space. The campground had been set up in a natural clearing in the trees. A spring-fed creek wandered along one edge. The trees and underbrush were thicker on the opposite side, which probably explained why the man had taken off in that direction. Jesse guessed there might be as many as a dozen people squatting in the camp. He couldn't be sure, as he had no way of knowing how many of the crude shelters served more than one person.

The man reappeared and Jesse started to leave the cover of the trees when his peripheral vision captured movement at the other end. A young woman stepped into the clearing and paused as if she wasn't sure where she was or why she'd managed to be there. She looked over her shoulder and began to pivot, as if to retreat. The man saw her and said something to her that Jesse couldn't hear. She spun back toward the voice and her mouth popped open. Would she run? The man took three long-legged steps toward her and was nearly on her when she turned and tried to run. He grabbed her wrist. She started to scream and he put his hand over her mouth. Jesse strode out from cover and drew his pistol.

"Hold it right there, Mister," he said in his best lieutenant's voice. It had been a while he'd used it but the edge was still there.

The man didn't let the girl go but whirled toward Jesse. He dropped his hand from the girl's mouth, spun her around and crossed her chest with his left arm, his hand grasping a fistful of frock. He held her that way, her back to him, and pulled her tight against him. He jerked a knife from his belt with the other hand, and held it against her throat. Jesse slid the receiver on the gun back, chambering a round, and pointed the pistol at a spot between the man's eyes.

"You take a step closer and I cut her," the man said. Close up, Jesse could see that he was older than he first thought, seemed unsteady on his feet, and had red rheumy eyes. Probably not going to be a problem. Jesse had spent time in the trenches in France. He'd seen frightened men up close, had dispatched a few, and, as a result, lived to see the war end.

"Mister, that don't make no sense. You use that knife and she drops. You don't have any cover and I shoot you dead. That's the first thing you need to think on. The second is, I got me a little piece of tin, courtesy of the U S of A Army, that says I am a dead shot with this little pea-shooter. I could put a bullet in your brain, whether you let her go or not."

"You cain't."

"Can do. Let her go 'fore I give you a third eye."

"Who in hell you think you are, Mister?"

"Just passing through, looking to get me some information. Let her go and we're even."

"You got a badge?"

"Nope. Let her go. I am dead serious about yanking this here trigger."

The man's eyes ricocheted about in their sockets. He glanced over his shoulder and pushed the girl at Jesse. She stumbled forward and Jesse caught her before she hit the ground. By the time he had her steady and on her feet, the man with the knife had disappeared. He could hear him crashing away through the forest. Well, there was an interview he wouldn't be making today. There was a real likelihood he'd be back to collect his stuff. Bums don't own much, but what they do own is important to them, so, yeah, he'd be back and the girl had better be gone.

"So, are you okay, Miss?"

"Yes, sir, I am. Thank'ee."

"It ain't none of my business, but what in the blazes are you doing in a place like this?"

"I reckon I could ask you the same."

"You could do. Who was that man and why was he ready to send your soul over?"

"I don't know. Never seen him afor. I come looking for Billy and they told me at the general store that if he was on the run, this is where I'd find him."

Jesse looked at the girl closely for the first time. She couldn't have been more than fifteen. Her dress was straight out of the Butterick catalog. Serena had one almost the same and he'd watched her cut the patterns and sew it into existence. Her hair was a mess. He thought he saw some straw in it which suggested she'd spent a night or two in a barn. She was on the run. A glance at her midriff told him why.

"Billy responsible for that?" he said and pointed at her bump that strained at the sash of her dress. The girl nodded and dropped her eyes.

"And let me guess, when your pa found out you were in a family way, and no Billy on the scene, he tossed you out."

She began to cry.

"Darlin' you are in a proper mess, ain't you? Okay, this ain't no place for you to be at. You sure you didn't know that fella just now?" The girl sniffed and shook her head. "And yet, you figured you'd just sashay in here and find your Billy, drop in on the parson, and everything would be hunky-dory."

"He said he loved me and we would get married."

"How long did you and Billy know each other?"

"Not long."

"He...what? He came through with a threshing crew and swept you off your feet and then he was gone?"

"How'd you know?"

"Sweetheart, you need to come with me. You ain't safe out here alone. Let me get you to my wife, she'll know what to do."

The girl hesitated.

"Or you can wait right here and see who come first, Billy or that rascal who had a mind to...never mind what he was up to."

She let him lead her away.

Chapter Ten

Serena frowned, but said nothing when Jesse ushered the girl into their kitchen. Jesse sat her down and poured a cup of coffee and put it on the table in front of her.

"You can start, Missy, by telling us your name."

The girl looked at the coffee cup, at Jesse, and at Serna. A tear rolled down one cheek, but she said nothing.

"Jess," Serena cut in, "you and me need a minute. Honey, there's some fried potatoes in the skillet if you're hungry and by the look of you, that would be a for-sure. You just get comfortable. We're your friends and you're safe here."

Serena pulled Jesse into the parlor. "You want to tell me what that messed up girl is doing in my house?"

Jesse described what had happened at the campsite and his fear that if he didn't pull her out, the girl would likely be dead by noon.

"That's laying it on pretty thick, Jesse. How can you know that?"

"When a no-good like that man puts a knife to a girl's throat, it's fair to say nothing good's going to happen anytime soon. Listen, Serena. Just let her rest up a bit. We'll find out who she is and see what we can do to keep her safe. Maybe her Billy will turn up and that'll be that."

"Jesse, for a smart man, you can now and again, for sure,

be a dunce. Billy is no more coming to find this girl than he's hankering for any of the other children he's ruined on his way through the countryside. He's a rounder and he's busy right about now sweet-talking another girl out of her virtue."

"Okay, maybe you're right, but I couldn't leave her there, could I? When she's settled and maybe sleeps for a time, we can figure out what comes next. I'll stop at Lawyer Bradford's on my way home and see what he has to say. There has to be something better'n being turned out for girls like that."

"There ought to be, but I'm thinking there isn't. The funny thing is, you know that if she were a mountain girl, she'd be married up with this Billy this minute. No way her pa would settle for anything less. He'd track down the boy and have him in front of a preacher in a heartbeat. It'd be what they're calling a shotgun wedding, but it would have happened. Down here in the 'civilized' world, she's just another throwaway. Okay, Jesse, your big heart and tiny brain will sooner or later fetch us up a bushel of trouble, but I wouldn't have it any other way. I'll get her settled and wait for you to get this figured out."

"Thank you. I gotta go."

"Not until you at least find out that girl's name and where she's from. If you aim to chat with Bradford, that's the first thing he's going to want to know."

"Oh, right. I will."

"And you'd better get that gun off your hip before you go prancing around town and the sheriff arrests you for terrorizing all the old ladies. You mountain men…I swear a body just can't let you out among the civilized people without a keeper."

By the time Jesse got to the mill, work seemed pretty much on schedule. He expected he owed that to Henry Sturgis. He walked into the office. R.G. sat where he always did and had on the same clothes he always wore. Jesse thought he must have ten identical shirts, pairs of trousers, and vests in his closet. The only difference he could recall from one day to the next was his necktie, if he wore one or not, and his collars, again, if he wore one or not.

"Where you been, Jesse? I was thinking I might have to send out a search party for you with one of them Saint Bernard dogs like they have in Switzerland or someplace over there in them mountains. Seems like Sturgis has the boys in line."

"Yes, sir, he does. He was a good hire." Jesse plunked down at the desk he used when not out in the yard and explained how it came he was late.

"You be careful out at that camp. Some of those drifters are Communists and worse. You take that man who would have assaulted the girl. Why, I reckon he was a Bolshevik."

"R.G., you can't possibly know that. He could have been a damned Republican just as easy. Besides, when did you all of a sudden get political? I never heard you go on like that before. Well, maybe a little when you talk about Teddy Roosevelt, sure, but otherwise? Never."

It was true. R.G. had always been the most tolerant man Jesse knew. He'd even hired Negroes from time to time, for crying out loud, and he never asked anything of his employees except if they were willing to work hard. Now, all of a sudden he'd got a bug in his ear about politicians and politics.

"It's bad enough that we're being asked to vote for a New York Damyankee and Catholic, to boot, candidate for President, but we got that traitor Norman Thomas running along with William Z. Foster, who is an out-and-out bomb-tossing Communist, by God."

"Thomas is a traitor?"

"Right along there with Foster, yes, sir. Socialist, Communist, all the same thing. Why, they want to take private businesses away from them that built them and give them to any lazy bum who raises his hand, like the do-nothings out at that camp."

"Well, that's a mite strong, don't you think? Some of them men is just down on their luck, as you can surely understand. Besides Mr. Hoover and his 'Chicken in every pot' is for sure going to sweep this election, ain't he?"

"We'll see. We certainly can't turn the country over to the Pope or the Bolshies."

"Not Al Smith, no. The boys up on the mountain are depending on Hoover to keep Prohibition going. Smith said he'd end it. No, sir, he ain't getting no votes off of Buffalo Mountain."

"Too right."

"You feeling okay, R.G.? You sure don't sound like your old self."

R.G.'s eyes seemed to glaze over. If he'd been fooling his mental slippage before, he sure wasn't now. R.G., the polite, reasonable man he once knew, the man who gave him the chance to get off the mountain, had been dropped into a brand new place. It made Jesse sad to see it.

R.G.'s eyebrows came together and he shook his head. "What? Me, okay? Well, sure enough. Say, you ought to tell what happened out there with those bums to the sheriff. If one of them will attack an innocent girl there, he might try again in town or anyplace. We should send them packing back to wherever they came from."

So, maybe R.G. had returned to the present. Jesse was relieved and worried at the same time. Buying the mill before some out-of-state swindler grabbed it looked more and more a good play.

"Tell the sheriff, yes. I would...I will, but not before I have a chance to talk to the men out there. I am probably wasting my time doing it, but I need to find out if any of them remember the one-eyed man from back in ought-eighteen."

"Oh, yeah, you asked me if I remembered his name. Did I tell you? Brown, I think. Well, you be careful out there, son."

Chapter Eleven

Bradford's eyebrows climbed a half inch and he shrugged when he heard Jesse's story. The future of Amy Cates, though murky and sad, did not produce in him a positive response or, worse, any useful advice. "These girls are going to get themselves in trouble one way or t'other and that is a sad fact. I don't know why they can't keep their bloomers up when some bad boy comes around, but there it is."

"Mister Bradford, don't the boy have some responsibility here? This girl can't be more'n fifteen if she's a day. She's a child. How is she going to know how to deal with a growed-up man with an itch?"

"Jesse, don't take this wrong, but you come off Buffalo Mountain not so long ago. Tell me honestly, what would you say is the average age of new brides up there? Fifteen, sixteen? Isn't it true that some of them might even be married off at fourteen?"

"It ain't the same."

"No? How's that?"

"The mountain is like a…whatsis…a community. Everybody knows everybody. They know their business, who's doin' what to who, who sparking their daughters, and nigh on to everything else. Girls might be ruined up there just like down here, only there is a consequence. On the mountain, if you take a girl's virtue, you marry up with her. It's as simple as B comes after A.

That's how it's different. Down here, where folks come and go and hardly anybody knows anybody else more'n two blocks away, girls and even boys can get lost. Nobody cares much if they do, unless it's their own kin, and even then, maybe not."

"That is as may be, but the point I want to make is this, every one of the women and girls up in your mountain knows exactly what happens when you let yourself go. It ain't no secret what's likely to happen. Same as here. That girl you got sitting in your kitchen knew what could happen if she led him on. You said it first, there are consequences and I agree. That's all I'm saying."

"That might be the lawyer way to look at it. I ain't no legal scholar, but it seems to me that man or woman, if you're willing to make a baby, you ought to be willing to raise it. If you don't want the responsibility, keep your britches on 'til you're growed-up and ready. See that is the difference 'tween here and the mountain. It ain't so much a thing about age as it is about you willing to pick up your share of the load. Sometimes that comes at you sooner than you had in mind, but once done, you step up."

"Well, if you say so. Either way, I got nothing for you. Now, in places like Richmond and maybe Roanoke, there are homes for unwed mothers where they put them up until the baby is born and then ship it off to be adopted. You could look for something like that."

"Maybe. I don't know. Let me ask you this, if that girl was to sue this Billy boy for support or maybe…what do you call it…breach of promise, would a judge rule for her? Remember, I'm saying if."

"I am not a judge and don't aim to be one, so I don't know. Also, with no Billy on the scene, what good would it do? And finally, the bigger problem is, where's she going to find a lawyer who'd file the suit?"

"Well, on the first one, if she won, she'd have something to nail the boy down next he come around and why couldn't you be that lawyer?"

"Me? Oh, no you don't, Jesse. We have a nice arrangement here, so don't you go ruining it with figuring me to do *pro bono* work that will only get the judge mad at me and take up time for a zero outcome."

"Well, I think you are the man to do it. That's all. Okay, the other thing I wanted to check in with you about is the one-eyed fella we're looking for. You had any luck?"

"No luck there. Not yet, anyway. I put in a call to some folks I know who keep track of those things, but nothing yet. Are you going back out to that campsite?"

"I reckon I am."

"You oughtn't go alone. Unless I am losing my touch, you got one of them bindlestiffs mad enough at you already to stick a knife in your ribs. Also, he'll have talked to the others and you might find yourself in a situation that could turn sour in a heartbeat, as my old daddy would say."

"Maybe yes, maybe no. I had a good look in the eyes of that jasper. There wasn't no fight in them. I been taking the measure of men set to pull a trigger or a knife on you most of my life in one place or another. This old boy is not a problem that way. It's most probable he's packed up and gone away by now. If he hasn't, I'm thinking he'll not have said anything to the others. I reckon they have him pegged pretty right as to who and what he is already and they won't be acting on his say-so. Not today they won't."

"You're the war hero. If you say it, I believe it. Only, if it was me, I'd take some help with me out there. Good luck."

· ● ● ● ·

Jesse's watch read six-thirty when he stepped into the clearing for a second time. There were more men this time. A half dozen that he could see, how many more were hunkered down in shacks and tents, he couldn't say. He checked to make sure his gun was loose in its holster and approached the man closest to him. The man turned and shouted.

"Hey, rube!"

The other men turned toward Jesse. Some bent down and picked up firewood. Others' hands went to their pockets.

"Easy now. This ain't no circus and I ain't looking for no trouble."

"You the man that chased off Elroy?"

"If he was a tall, scrawny man who liked to hurt little girls, yeah, that would be me."

The men relaxed, but still held onto their makeshift clubs.

"What you want?"

"Information, is all. You all get around, I take it. I was wondering if, in your travels, you run across a one-eyed man, maybe looked like he mighta been from a better place one time."

"Except for the one eye, that could be any one of us. Why do you want to find him? You a copper?"

"Nope. See, a bunch of years ago, this man who sported a glass eye delivered a message to my ma about my pa being dead from the Spanish flu. Well, it turns out that wasn't true. So, either he had something to do with my pa being robbed and killed or he was working for who did and he could maybe lead me to that man."

A short man wearing bib overalls a size too big for him said, "That sounds like Brownie."

"Brownie? His name was Brown?"

R.G. had it right. Who knew?

"It's what we called him." The first man said. "You said he might be mixed up in a murder? Is that what you're hinting at?"

"Pretty much, yeah. I can't say he done it or knew firsthand. He might have and he might not. Did he help rob my pa and split the takings with someone else? Did he do it himself? Or was he just a bum someone, maybe the guy who done it, hired to tell my ma a story?"

A third man stepped up. "Name is Kick, William Kick. I knew of this man a time back. I don't know him well, yes? But I don't think he's a man to hurt anybody, you see?"

"Okay. That an opinion or do you have something else?" The man shook his head.

"I can accept that. Anybody else here know about this here Brownie?"

The short man held out a dirty hand. "Simon Wade," he said. "Last I saw of that man, if it were him, was over in Tennessee, only he didn't have no glass eye then. He was wearing a patch over the eye like some damned pirate. Said he was heading north and try to catch on with a threshing crew late. You a farmer? No? Okay, so them crews by the time they hit Pennsylvania or New York are tired and homesick. Lots of them collect their pay and skedaddle. Crew boss can't be too particular who they take on by then. That's when folks like us can get some work."

A fourth man stepped out of the deepening shadows. "I can tell you this much, Mister, you ain't going to find Brownie, if that's his name. He's dead. A bunch of us were cleaning up a wheat field late two years ago. Brownie had the job of catching the straw off the McCormick reaper. Straw boss had been riding him all day. He finally said something and that old Brownie come down off that wagon with a pitchfork in his hand like he was going to poke it into the boss' guts. Well, the boss, he just laughed, stepped to one side, and tripped Brownie. He, you know, flailed his arms around and landed facedown. Somehow, he come down on that fork and stabbed his own self in the heart. Deader'n a chunk. If you be aiming to talk to him, you can forget it, sure."

A dead end.

"Well, thanks for the information. Say, why ain't you all working?"

"That's a bad joke, Bub. We ain't working 'cause nobody is hiring. Everybody is too busy getting rich to take you on permanent."

"Any of you know sawmills or steam engines?"

"I spent some time in a laundry," Kick said. "Tended to the steam belt system."

"Could you repair one if you had to?"

"I think I could."

"Come to the mill tomorrow morning and if you're telling the truth, you'll have yourself a job."

Chapter Twelve

Serena had that look on her face that Jesse knew meant he was in trouble. Not the "who ate the last piece of pie?" kind of trouble, but the chilly days and frosty nights kind. The lamps were lit and his dinner sat on the kitchen table—cold. Amy Cates was nowhere in sight and he could hear the children in the bedrooms upstairs fussing about something. Serena sat stone-faced in the corner with her nose in a book. Jesse started to say something when little Adeline wheeled around the door jamb, eyes brimming with tears and dragging Mister Roosevelt, her stuffed bear, by one paw.

"Pa, Tommy says that when I grow up I'll have to marry some flatlander and live in town and raise a passel of babies and do the wash and everything. I said I wasn't going to ever get married and besides if I did, I would marry you. He said I couldn't do either of them things."

"Of *those* things," Serena corrected.

"Of those things. That's not true, is it? Tell Tommy he's a wicked liar."

"Wicked? Where'd you learn that word, Addie girl?"

"Miss Amy said it. She said you chased off a wicked man and saved her life. Is that true? Did you save Miss Amy's life?"

"No, I just convinced a bad man—"

"A wicked man?"

"Okay, maybe a little wicked. I just persuaded him, you could say, to find himself some other part of the county to plant his boots."

"Your daddy is very brave, Addie. Now get yourself off to bed. You won't be marrying anybody anytime soon, so you got nothing to worry about, honey." Serena gave her daughter a little shove and sent her on her way. "You tell Tommy if he doesn't stop pestering you, Pa is going to come up there and give his bottom a proper tanning."

They listened to Addie and Mister Roosevelt thump up the stairs and deliver the message. They could hear Tommy mumble something that sounded like "tattletale tit" and then all was quiet.

"You want to tell me where you were 'til dark time, Jess? You do remember you left me here with a bit of damaged goods and no plan as to what I was to do with her?"

Jesse held up his hands in surrender and nodded. He described his day including Bradford's gloomy assessment of Amy's situation. He also related his second visit to the tramp camp and what he'd learned, including the fact that the one-eyed man, whose nickname turned out to be Brownie, was dead. They both sat in silence for a moment. Jesse picked at his meal. Serena made it clear she had no intention of heating it up. Jesse said it was fine just the way it was. Cold pork chops and cabbage was just dandy, but maybe a dab of ketchup on the fried potatoes might just pep them up a bit. Serena shoved the bottle across the table at him.

"So, where's she at, Serena?"

"The girl? I fed her, gave her a good scrubbing, put her in a fresh nightgown, and settled her in on a pallet in the pantry. It ain't much, but I don't want her bunking in with the children. Poor soul ate like she hadn't a meal in a week and she did need a bath bad. She was asleep the minute her head hit the pillow. She's just a child, Jesse, not a woman. She's barely seven years older than Tommy, for pete's sake. She should be home learning to bake cookies and to sew, not giving birth to a baby. Laws, it's children having children nowadays. I don't know but it seems to me that girls grow up slower down here than on the mountain. So, Bradford had nothing to say?"

"Nope. I even asked him if she might have a legal case, could she sue Billy whatever his name is. I heard on R.G.'s radio where some woman up in New York City sued this rich man who said he'd marry her, only he changed his mind. It was called 'breach of promise.' You ever hear of such a thing?"

"Like to see some rich high-roller pull something like that up on the mountain."

"He'd find himself staring at the business end of a scatter gun 'fore nightfall."

They sat in silence for a minute. Jess pushed the cabbage around on his plate as if he thought prodding it might bring it back to life.

"Jess, what are we going to do with the girl?"

"I know it's a burden, Serena, but there ain't no plan for girls who get themselves in a family way like she done. I don't know much about them things, but I do hear stories and, in fact, I seen some of them myself when I was in the Army before we shipped out. They die or end up on the streets doing what no God ever intended them to be doing at that young age, so I just know I can't put her back on the street."

"They were doxies?"

"That would be a polite way of putting it, yep. Walking the streets and…Serena, they looked like old women and they were just youngsters, some of them. Listen, we can't be the ones who put her into that life. I don't know what we can do, but I won't do that."

Serena looked at him, waiting.

"It ain't like we got the time, money, or room to take her on, but how about we give her a little space before she sets out again?"

"You mean, let her stay here a while? How long?"

"Danged if I know. A week…two?"

Serena sat back and closed her eyes. Jesse imagined she was calculating the costs in time, extra food to be prepared, explanation to the neighbors and the children. He'd seen that posture back when she did R.G.'s books at the mill. Her hands would dance over the keys of her adding machine and then she'd twist the crank, push more keys, and pretty soon she'd sit back and write a number on a scrap of paper.

She looked up. She'd finished her sums, it seemed.

"Here's what I think we can do, Jess. It isn't perfect, but it'll work for now. You know I have a backlog of work for R.G. sitting on my table along with the sewing and mending I can't get to, and our own money to sort out. I can pretty much keep up with the household, but the only reason I still got a paycheck coming in is because R.G. is forgetful on the one hand and generous on the other. So, this girl can stay a spell on this condition. She isn't a guest. She pulls her weight. She can look after the children. When the older ones are off to school, she takes care of the others. She does chores, helps with the cooking and cleaning, and keeps herself in order."

"Like she was one of our own."

"Well, that might be a stretch. Jess, she is a child, like we agreed, so we're going to see to it that she gets to be one a while longer. There has got to be an answer out there somewhere for her situation and it will find us, if we're patient. I'm with you. I don't want to be the one responsible for sending this girl out into the kind of life where it appears she's headed if something isn't done."

"Okay. That will have to do. I will see if I can find one of them unwed mother places nearby, or maybe track down her parents. I can't believe they forced her to leave home. What kind of people would do that to their own blood?"

"Some folks is hard, Jesse. You know that as much as anybody. Now, hand me that plate. Let me heat the food up a mite. You get all bound up in your insides eating cold potatoes and ketchup like that."

"You're a good person, Serena."

"You're the one who dragged that stray puppy home."

Chapter Thirteen

William Kick showed up at the mill as he said he would. The main gate swung open and the workmen filed in. He followed them in, hesitated, unsure of what he should do next, and then spotted Jesse. He smiled, probably relieved, and worked his way over to him.

"Well, Mister Kick, are you ready to tackle our tired old steam engine?"

"I think maybe, yes. What is the problem?"

"Like I said, it just seems all tuckered out, like maybe it's old and ready to go home and sit on the porch, like old men do."

"What?"

"Sorry, I was being poetical, I guess. It don't have the power it used to. It will turn and move the belt along until there's some push-back, and then it huffs but can't always get the saw blade spinning like it should."

"Maybe you show it to me?"

"Yep, right this way."

Jesse led him over to the vertical single-cylinder steam engine. Without any work being done, the flywheel spun and the belt around it flapped along. But when the sawyer threw the lever that put tension on it and sent a log sliding down the rails and into the saw, the engine strained and the blade's revolutions slowed. It seemed that if the log had been green or old oak, it wouldn't have cut at all. With tulip wood, however, it still sliced through the log on the carrier, but at an agonizingly slow rate.

"You see what I mean?"

"I got no tools. You have some? I can fix this for now. Maybe then you can talk about what happens to this engine in the future."

Jesse led William to the toolshed. He searched among the tools, shoved some into his pockets, grabbed a few more, and walked over to the still-huffing machine.

"First, we must shut this one down." He turned off the valve that led to the boiler. The saw grabbed at the wood and stopped spinning. "You should back that log out, I am thinking. Good, so now we exhaust what steam is in the system and den we fix him, yes?"

Steam whistled from the blow-out valve and William applied wrench and hammer to the cylinder.

"So, here is your problem. You know how this fella works, yes?" Jesse, shrugged. Maybe he did and maybe he didn't. "So there is dis intake valve here where the steam comes in. It pushes the piston down. Den, dis little cog here pushes against this rod and boop, dat valve is closing and the exhaust valve, he is opening. So, in...out. As long as the wheel she spins, puff, puff. Now after a while, dose valves that put the steam in and out, dey get worn and so steam is leaking, both in and out, you see? So, you lose power. Just now, I turn a nut here and it puts more tension on springs that hold dem down when supposed to be. So, no leaking. Now, we turn open the line to the boiler, let her get going and...okay, now saw that log."

Sure enough, the blade spun and sang through the log. No stalling, no loss of power.

"Cutting like through warm butter. William, you got yourself a job. Say, can you do the same thing with them gas engines?"

"Yah, sure."

"Okay, let's get into the office and get you signed up. By the way, it ain't none of my business, but where'd that accent come from all of a sudden?"

"What?"

"You sound like some of them Fritzies I had the honor of shooting at during the war."

William stopped in his tracks. "I didn't know it…that must explain it."

"What?"

"Is a long story. I am German immigrant. I came here as a boy with my parents."

"Kick ain't exactly a German name."

"That's just it. We come through Immigration Office and man says 'What's your name?' My father says it and man says, 'Write it down. So he does. Our name was Kük. That's a K and a U with an umlaut, K. You know what is an umlaut?"

"Nope."

"It's two dots over the letter. Well, when my father writes it, this man in immigration doesn't know either and he sees what looks like two I's, you know with little dots. So he says, 'You're Kiik? Then he says 'yep" prints Kiik on our documents. So we are no longer Kük, but Kiik. We change what we can. Only one I and add a C. So, I am this boy named Kick. A German boy who, when the war comes, must be a spy. My father's bakery is damaged by men in masks. I join the Army, fight in France, but still, I am the first one laid off. So, that's why you find me in the camp and why, when I don't think about how I sound, the accent sneaks out."

"Well, that's a lot more'n I needed to know, but probably everything I should. Let's get you on the payroll so's you can start paying Mister Wilson's income tax."

• • ● ● •

When the whistle blew for lunch, Jesse sought out William. "How's she going, Willie?"

"Willie? No, please not that. I am born Wilhelm, but William, now. Willie is what we called the Kaiser, remember?"

"I do and that were a spell back. You don't need to worry none about that."

"With this sometimes accent, maybe I do. Jesse, there is something I need to tell you. I thought maybe I shouldn't, then, maybe I should."

"What?"

"You remember that man you chased away/"

"You all called him Elroy?"

"Him. He came back last night. He asked what you wanted and we told him. This morning, when he found out I was coming here, he said to tell you he had something to say to you about a killing ten years ago. That was what you were asking about, yes?"

"Yeah."

"He said to tell you he might have a line on who done the killing and if you came by this evening, he could tell you. He said you should bring a five-dollar bill, though."

"Five?"

"That's what he said."

●　●　⬤　●　●

Jesse managed to scrape together five dollars in paper and silver. Some he borrowed from R.G., some from Henry Sturgis. He said he'd pay them back on payday. Elroy must have got into his head that Jesse had more money than he did. He guessed men living on the edge could make that mistake. The forest had turned dark. Jesse patted the service piece on his hip and walked toward the camp.

Elroy met him at the verge. "You bring the money?"

"I did."

"Hand it over here."

"Whaen I hear what you got to say."

"Money or no words."

"How about I put it on this here stump? It can sit there. You tell me what you got and if it's for real, I walk away and you pick it up. If it is some old guff, I pick it up and you walk away."

"That ain't the deal."

"It's the only one I'm making. Look at it, Elroy." Jesse deposited the coins and bills on the stump. "Cash money."

"Okay. I take that. Here's what I know about Brownie and the pol—"

Jesse recognized the rifle from which the shot had been fired. You don't spend the time in the trenches in the war and not know what an Lee-Enfield rifle sounds like. Elroy's hand froze in midair as he reached for the money. His eyes widened, as if he'd just won the jackpot at the state fair. He dropped to the ground and a bloodstain spread across his back.

Jesse stood completely still. He waited for the second shot. The one meant for him. It didn't come. What he heard was someone crashing away through the brush. Then, closer, and coming toward him.

Chapter Fourteen

No one would have to inspect Elroy's body to certify he was dead. There are some things you just know. The men from the camp crashed through the brush and surrounded Jesse.

Angry eyes, fearful eyes, questioning eyes bore in on Jesse.

"You shoot this man?"

Jesse couldn't be sure which of them spoke. He put up his hands, looked to his right hip, and slowly reached for his pistol. He pulled it free from its holster with his thumb and forefinger and handed it to William, who took it and pressed it against his own neck.

"Cold," he said

Then he pulled back the receiver and ejected a bullet. He held the slide back, inserted his thumb into the chamber and stared down the barrel. The light was fading, but there was enough for him to see.

"This gun has not been fired. Jesse did not shoot this man." He handed the gun and bullet back to Jesse. Jesse tucked the bullet into his vest pocket and holstered the gun.

"Why would I? He claimed he had some news about the one-eyed man to tell me. He told William here that he'd tell me what that was for five dollars. See, it's setting there on that tree trunk. That there is a heap of money, but I'd pay it if the news was any good. Anyway, he was about to tell me something and... well, there he is."

"What did he tell you?" Simon Wade asked.

"That's just it. He didn't say anything worth knowing. He sure didn't earn his five dollars. Somebody put a bullet in him just as he was opening his mouth."

The men mumbled and poked at dead Elroy. "So, what are you aiming to do now, Mister?"

"Do?" Jesse scratched his head. "Well, before I fetch the police, I reckon I'll take me a look at what he mighta had on him. Here, give me a hand rolling him over."

Jesse searched Elroy's pockets. He had a dirty handkerchief, a nickel, two cigarette stubs with what a bum might consider some smoking left in them, and a pocket knife with one broken blade. He rocked back on his heels. "Not much here."

"There's something wrote on his cuff."

Sure enough, written on the cuff, almost lost in grime, in shaky cursive that looked as if it had been written with a piece of charcoal out of the fire and smudged near to the point of illegibility, someone had scrawled what might have been fp—8. Maybe.

"What do you suppose that means?"

"Could be some jasper's initials? He was working that farm over on the river and he was supposed to feed pigs at eight."

"Feed pigs at eight? Marvin, you are a dope."

"Well, I'm just saying. You got something better, Simon, spit it out."

"Forget it. Listen, Mister, calling in the sheriff ain't such a good idea. You do that and we all might all end up in the pokey. The sheriff ain't too happy with us being here in the first place and would be more than happy to toss us for killing Elroy."

"But you didn't."

"Don't matter. He will be ready to close out a murder and this camp all at the same time."

Jesse reached over and picked up the money. He shoved all but two dollars into his pants pocket. "Here's what I think you all should do. There is a pretty decent hash house back down the road a piece. Whyn't you all take this two dollars and grab a bite of supper, maybe have a piece of pie—there's pretty good pie at that place—and have a chat about what ought to be done. After all, it's your patch, ain't it?"

The men looked at one another, seemed to grasp what Jesse had in mind, and shuffled off with Jesse's two dollars in hand. He watched them leave. He'd done the right thing, he hoped. There was no doubt in his mind that if the sheriff were called in, best case, these men would be dispossessed, their shelters destroyed and they'd be scattered. Worst case, well, Simon had put it pretty straight. Homeless men, bums like them, had no standing in this post-war economic extravaganza. He watched them disappear into the evening gloom.

● ● ● ● ●

Jesse took his time driving home. Serena was going to have a duck fit what with him being late for supper again, but he needed to get some thinking done before he tackled her and all that he had to deal with at home. For example: there was the rifle shot. It had been dead on target. That is, if the shooter wanted Elroy dead, it was. Pretty bad, if he wasn't and the man had been aiming at Jesse. So, which? Then there was the thing about the reload. Jesse heard the shooter pulling the bolt back and a new shell put into the chamber. It had been a distance away, for sure, and there were some who'd doubt anybody's hearing could be that good, but there're some things you never forget and cocking an Lee-Enfield was one of them. In the Army, firing a rifle had a fixed sequence that was drummed into your head all through basic training: squeeze the trigger, rack back the bolt to eject the shell, and ram it forward to chamber the next. Locked and loaded, ready to fire again. Never varied.

He'd heard that sequence out there in the woods. Did that mean the shooter was fixing to fire again…at him? Or was it a matter of habit? Was the shooter an Army man? That was something to ponder on. Then, what would the men do?

Jesse felt pretty sure that by the time the men finished their pie and coffee, they'd agree that a dead Elroy would be best found a mile or two away from the camp and by somebody else. It might take a day or even a week before that happened. To Jesse, that decision would make sense if he were up on the mountain. Down here in the valley, he wasn't so sure.

He gave the car some gas. It was time to get on home.

• ● **●** ● •

Contrary to what he expected, Serena seemed almost cheerful. True, his supper sat on the kitchen table, cold as stone, instead of on the warming tray, but here was hot coffee and a pie cooling on the windowsill.

"I expect you will tell me what kept you this time. You know your children are like to forget what you look like if you keep this up."

"Sorry. So I will tell you everything you need or want to know, but you tell me how'd it go today with Amy and all?"

"Amy? Well, she did just fine after I explained to her that we weren't a charity ward at some home for strays. I told her she could stay or go as she saw fit, but if she left, there was no coming back. That's one, and then I reckoned the likelihood her Billy was heading this way searching for her was pretty slim. She cried a little about that. I also told her if this Billy really wanted to marry her, he'd find a way here and she'd be smarter staying put so he could, instead of gallivanting all over creation looking for him."

"Sounds about right."

"Then I told her that if she stayed, she'd need to do her share of the chores. After she had her cry, she dressed herself and pitched right in. That pie you're eyeing like you used to look at me is her doing. So, what kept you?"

Jesse told her what had happened, that the man had been killed before he'd been able to say anything, and what he guessed the men would do.

"Where'd you get five dollars?"

"That's all you're going to ask me about?" Okay, I had some pocket money, as you surely know. I borrowed the rest from R.G. and Henry down at the mill."

"Five dollars! And you gave away two to those bums?"

"I did. Serena, a man was shot dead. The shooter mighta been aiming at me. If they had not come crashing up when they did, I could have been next. I heard him chamber another round into a rifle, which in the right hands is known to be damn near deadly at three hundred yards. Don't that give you pause?"

"You could have been shot?"

"Well, yeah."

"Then you need to stop all this crime-fighting. You let Sheriff Privette figure this out like he said."

"He ain't about to do a dad-burned thing, Serena. Not a dad-burned thing."

"So he doesn't. Are you thinking me being a widow woman and your children orphans is the way to go?"

"No, but—"

"Eat your dinner. I'm going to bed."

"You can be a handful of hot coals, sometimes."

"Jesse, listen to me. Your pa got killed ten years ago, right? And the only lead you had was a one-eyed man who you now know is dead. A man come along and says, 'For five dollars, I can solve this mystery for you,' and you think it's worth it. Now he's dead, too. Where are you going with this? Jesse, I am serious. I don't want you dead. We been down that path once before. You think on that for a spell. Like I said…good night."

Chapter Fifteen

Amy Cates spooned out grits and added a slab of bacon and a slice of bread she'd toasted over the open flame of the stove. She didn't say a word to Jesse, but he could tell she'd gotten ahold of herself and seemed, if not happy, then content. Serena watched her the way a schoolteacher keeps tabs on a student. She seemed to be okay with Amy's performance so far.

"I'll be visiting the library they opened up last week, Jess. You want me to pick you up some reading?"

"Something to read? Me? Um, maybe. See if you can find me a book on watches. Pocket watches."

"You want a book about pocket watches, like the history of them or…what?"

"I don't know, exactly. I guess I want to know if there is a market for old watches and if so, where it's at."

"You're wanting to find out how and if you can track down your pa's watch."

"Yep."

"I'll look and ask whoever is in charge, but I don't think you should get your hopes up on that. I thought you were done putting yourself in danger looking for your pa's killer."

"I ain't risking nothing by poking around in a book for news about a watch, now am I?"

"Only if someone who has a certain watch finds out. Then

it won't matter if your interest is just in the book or something else. Jesse, please let it go. All you're going to do is, best—waste your time and money. That, we've already seen you already did with dropping two whole dollars to feed a bunch of bums. Worst, you'll draw out someone who will shoot you 'fore they'll get themselves caught, and you could end up facing the business end of a bullet."

"Serena, you ain't even found me a book and already you got me shot dead." He turned to Amy who sat with her head bowed at the end of the table. "Amy, what do you think? You understand how it is to have to get something settled and off your chest once an' for all. Should I keep after a man who killed my pa or should I let it go? It's been ten years."

"Mister Jesse, I don't rightly know."

"Good answer there, Amy," Serena said. "Because Jesse don't rightly know, either, but he is so mule-headed, he won't let it go and that's a fact. I swear he won't live to see thirty the way he's going. Okay, Jess, I will ask about a book. I'll see if they have one on planning your own funeral while I am at it. You could get a grave dug out proper in the backyard so's there's no fuss and no bother. Just dump you in and shovel in the dirt."

"Lordy, it's just a book, Serena. I thought you'd be happy with me sticking to book learning than asking questions of strangers. I mean, suppose there is a place where these watches is traded around? After all, the Onion were a pretty historical watch and—"

"Historical? Your daddy was toting a famous watch?"

"It was not famous, no, but it had two things about it that somebody who likes old things and maybe collects them might could be interested in. It had a Jefferson Davis Guard medal stuck on the chain, for one. There weren't many of them given out. And two, it was from the old A M and O."

"You think there is a man out there somewhere who is looking for an old railroad watch and a Civil War medal and this book is going to lead you to him?"

"I give up with you, Serena. What in Holy Ned happened to the sweet mountain girl I married? This new one has got all spiky. Looks like I done traded a wildflower for a thistle."

"Jesse, that isn't fair. I just don't want you dead. Is that asking too much?"

Jesse started to say something sharp but stopped. He'd caught sight of what he could only suppose was a tear starting its slide down her cheek.

"It's okay, Serena, darlin'. I don't need a watch book. Maybe you can find me something about furniture-making. That'd be helpful, yep. So, you all take care. I gotta get going to the mill. R.G. is going to be thinking I'm what you're so het up about and lying dead in my bed."

• ● ● ● •

Jesse stuck his head in the office door and waved at R.G. before he headed to the yard to check up on how things were going. The ringing of saw blades slicing through logs and the sour odor of sawdust greeted him as he worked his way among the men. He found William up to his elbows in the inner workings of one of the tractors.

"Jesse, this old girl needs a good overhaul. Also, if this machine ain't used for anything other than driving that saw, it'd be better if we dismounted the engine from the tractor and bolted her down permanent to a platform. More room it be giving and better performance like that single-cylinder steamer we got."

"I'll check with the yard hands. If they don't ever use it to drag logs across the yard, we'll give that some real thought. Boy, things is really moving here. Am I seeing this aright? Is them blades turning faster?"

"Yeah, they are. See, what needed being done is grease on the axles of all the pulleys and idlers and I spent last night with a file and some of the boys and we sharpened all of them, yah."

"Well, my friend, you got yourself a one hundred percent permanent job. You're the maintenance man."

William grinned and shuffled his feet. "We got them blades pretty sharp, alright, but there's one or two with pretty bad skew in them. They been worked hot and dull, and they are not all flat and dere is some teeth missing. You should be looking for new ones, Jesse."

"I'll talk to R.G. Now about Elroy…?"

"I don't believe I know anybody with that name, do you?"

"I mighta done at one time or t'other. What do you suppose woulda happened to him, iffen I did know such a man?"

"Hard to say. So much confusion these days. I hear folks who stray from the straight and narrow more often than not end up badly. Why, I heard a rumor just this morning that someone with a name like that was found shot dead over by the railroad spur that runs by the big ice house. But that is only what people are saying, and I am not so sure the name was Elroy."

"Dangerous times, for sure. A man can't be too careful."

"No, sir, he can't. Oh, here's a piece of news. Simon found a place in the woods near where we stay where someone must have sat and had a smoke. He also found a spent bullet shell out there. Says he thinks it came from an Lee-Enfield rifle. Like the ones we carried in the war. That's interesting, yes?"

Jesse nodded and retreated to the office. He needed to talk R.G. into buying some saw blades, it seemed. Before he could ask, R.G. held a scrap of paper to his nose and squinted at the writing on it."

"Jack Braddock," he said.

"Jack Braddock? Captain Jack Braddock?"

"I don't know about the Captain business, but that was what he said his name was. I wrote it down. He must have stopped by your house, and Serena sent him here, and while he was here the phone rings, and by damn, it's for him. On a trunk line, long distance, I reckon. Don't ask me how he got a call out here, but he did and said he had to scoot. He said he'd find you tomorrow, maybe next week. Said it was important."

"Jack Braddock came all the way down here from Washington, DC, dropped in this office, got himself a phone call, and left? He said he had something important to say and he left?"

"That's what I just said, didn't I? Who the hell is Jack Braddock?"

"He was my company commander. We fought together ten years ago. I ain't seen him since we hit the port of New York City. Well, I'll be. And he didn't say nothing?"

"Nope. Say, Sturgis was in the Army with you back then, too, wasn't he?"

"Well, for a short piece he was. Why? Did Jack talk to him? Maybe he can tell me what the Captain wants."

"That's just it. Braddock looked over the yard, spotted Henry, turned away and when Henry was out of sight, he hopped in his Stutz and wheeled on out of here like a cat with turpentine on its rear end."

"Well, that is sure a poser, ain't it?"

Chapter Sixteen

Jesse drove into town during his lunch break. He'd told R.G. he had to check on some hardware in town and he'd use the time to do that. In fact he did need to order new files. William had worn out all of the old ones in what looked like a saw blade-sharpening jamboree with a dozen men working away on the lot.

After which Jesse thought he'd use the pretext of asking Sheriff Privette about the progress regarding his father's murder case to find out what the coroner might have found out about Elroy. He'd casually drop a word or two about bodies and see what the sheriff might drop.

He left the hardware store and by virtue of a lively sense of self-preservation developed during a childhood on Buffalo Mountain and service in the trenches of France managed to avoid bumping into Franklin P. Dalton, marching down the sidewalk with a face drawn into a heavy scowl. He looked like he was coming from the sheriff's office. Considering David Privette had called Franklin P. Dalton a disgrace to his office in Jesse's hearing only last Sunday, Jesse did have to wonder a little what business he might have there.

As he expected, Privette had nothing to say about Jesse's father's death. It was, as far as he was concerned "as cold as a witch's tit." As to other bodies that might have turned up in his jurisdiction, it was none of Jesse's business.

"You need to mind your own bee's wax, son, and leave policing to police."

"I ain't here to play at police, Sheriff. I happened to hear that another body turned up down at the ice house and thought that there was too much of a whatchacallit."

"Coincidence?"

"That."

"Well, since you asked. We do got us two bodies in this week. I swan, it never rains but it pours. I been in this job nine years and except for a man falling off a sidewalk and into the radiator of a speeding Chrysler automobile and a heart attack after a bar fight, we ain't had no dead people since just after the war. Well, 'course you know all about that. So, okay, up pops your pa and now some bum is shot dead down at the ice house. We no sooner get him on a slab in the morgue and they find a kid down by the creek outside the Henderson's back forty with a pitchfork stuck in his ribs. He was deader'n a chunk."

Those boys out at the camp hadn't wasted time moving Elroy's body. "Well, there you go, Sheriff. Taxpayers going to get their money's worth out of you this year. Bum have a name?"

"None we can find. You know these drifters, they travel light. My guess, he was running and got whoever it was that was after him, caught up. Now, the boy, him we can put a name to. Turns out we had a bulletin or two on him. Seems there's a passel of farmers with ruined daughters who'd like to have a sit-down with that boy, yes, sir. Too late now, though."

"Really? So…"

"So…so what? Oh, his name? There was one of them work cards found in his pocket. You know them kind that field crews use what say where and when to show up. Anyhow, it said his name was William Seymour. Henderson said he worked a crew on his place a while back and they called him Billy. Henderson said he was a smart aleck, if ever there was one and it don't surprise him none that he got himself skewered. I'm guessing he had his hands on the wrong girl this time and someone with a prior claim, you could say, removed him from the Romeo business."

"You're sure his name was Billy?"

"That's what they said. Seems he's been sparking young girls up and down the valley for a spell. It's amazing he lasted this long. Most of these old farmers are pretty quick on the trigger when it comes to their womenfolk."

"Whose pitchfork was it?"

"What? Whose pitchfork? Why'd I care about that?"

"Might lead you to his killer, don't you think?"

"Like I said, Jesse Sutherlin, you leave the policing to us, okay?"

"I hear you." Jesse got up. "Saw Dalton P. Franklin headed down the sidewalk in full steam as I came up."

Jesse left the sheriff's office, picked up a gross of files at the Mercantile, and headed back to the mill. So, it appeared Amy Cates was not going to get married to her Billy, after all. Poor kid. What happens to her now? No family, no future, and a baby on the way. How would he tell her? Maybe Serena should. Women are better at delivering bad news to other women than men, right?

And then he thought a bit on pitchforks. Dangerous things, pitchforks, whether you skewered yourself, as in Brownie's case, or were skewered by them with an angry father on the other end. If Jesse'd owned a pitchfork, he would have thrown it out first thing he got home.

● ● ● ● ●

Jesse decided to wait until after supper to tell Serena about Billy Seymour. Because Amy was not more than a child herself and carrying a baby, she would most likely drop off to bed about the same time as the children. He'd talk to Serena then. Between them, maybe they'd figure out what to do next. The night was mild. Serena pulled a shawl over her shoulders and followed Jesse out onto the back porch. She took the rocking chair. Jesse plunked himself down on the wood box and leaned back.

"Sometimes I wonder why they even bothered to put a front porch on this house. I seems like we never sit out there."

"If we lived closer in town, we might. It's a neighborly thing to do. Thing is, we ain't got no close neighbors out this way, and who wants to sit out front of an evening and watch automobiles and wagons go by? Serena, listen, I got some bad news to tell you."

"Oh, Jesse, what have you got yourself into now?"

"Whoa, hold up there. This ain't nothing to do with me. I swear, Serena, the way you go on. I reckon if I had been near the ocean, you'd have blamed me for sinking the *Titanic*."

"That's silly. You were only twelve then, and barely getting started in your meddlesome ways. Come to think of it, you were seventeen 'bout the time the war got going. You want to explain that?"

"I ain't never going to get a slack rein from you, am I?"

"Be in my best interest not to give you one."

Jesse sighed and sat all the way back. The shingle siding dug into his back. Where to begin? Well, he for sure wasn't going to mention Elroy. No need for that. The sheriff wasn't going looking and Serena didn't need to know.

"They found Amy's beau dead over by Henderson the farmer's creek."

"What?"

"The boy Amy is waiting for to come and marry her is dead. Somebody, someone he crossed, I guess, stabbed him with a pitchfork. Marriage with her baby's pa is off the table."

"Oh, laws. What'll she do now?"

The two sat in silence for a few minutes and then started speaking at once.

"We can't…"

"She'll have to…"

"You go."

"Jesse, she's got no place to go. What will happen to her? She's just a baby herself."

"There's some would say, if you're old enough to make a baby, you're old enough to take care of yourself."

"That's just hard man talk. Men, they come around, sweet talk some innocent thing out of her virtue, and then blame the upshot on the girl. There ought to be law that says, if you make it, you raise it that goes for the men, too."

"Never happen, darlin'."

"Right. It's a man's world and that means that responsibility for babies, making and raising and tending them, is a woman's work. It's not fair, Jesse. That girl probably had no more idea what she was getting herself into than a bunny. That boy, Billy, though, he did and run off the second he found out there was a bun in the oven. How many other girls did he do that to, I wonder?"

"Sheriff said there were some bulletins, so more'n one, I reckon."

"It's not right."

They sat in silence for a while longer. Serena shivered.

"I'm feeling a chill, Jess. There isn't a thing you or I can do about that girl tonight. We'll have to sleep on it and talk some more in the morning. Amy will have to be told. That'll be your job." She stood and walked into the kitchen."Come to bed and keep me warm."

Chapter Seventeen

Sunday mornings had a rhythm all their own—unlike school mornings which were filled with last-minute rushing around, lost books, shoes, and coats. Only little Adelaide would sail through that confusion. She had no school or kindergarten obligations to attend to. She could dawdle over her breakfast or not. In the midst of the hurly-burly, she'd rather pepper her parents with endless questions, almost all of which were preceded by, "Why?" And Saturdays were relaxed up to the point when chores were assigned and the week's schoolwork reviewed. But Sundays were different. Only preparing four children for church and getting them fed cluttered Serena's otherwise smooth execution of a day lacking multiple choices. Of course, there would be Sunday dinner to prepare and serve by one in the afternoon, and there was the weekly trip up the mountain to manage, but compared to a weekday, Sunday was a relative picnic. And now she had Amy Cates to help her.

The Sutherlins, children and adults, were arrayed around the kitchen table. Serena said the grace and stood to retrieve the pot of grits from the stove. She ladled out a portion for each. Tommy asked if they could have butter on them this time. It was Sunday, after all, and wasn't that a special day for Jesus? Wouldn't He be in favor of butter?

"Butter," Serena said. "Tommy, for what a pound of butter

cost, I could 'most buy you a new pair of sneakers like you saw in the catalog. You need those more'n you need butter on your grits. Black gravy is good enough. Amy, maybe you can whip up the gravy."

"Ma'am?"

"You know how to make gravy?"

"No'm, I'm afraid I don't. W'ere I come from, we don't have gravy much at all, not on our grits, anyway."

"Lord have mercy. Sorry, Lord, for breaking number three on your day. Girl, grits ain't no good without gravy. Everybody knows that."

"Yes'm."

"Come here. I'll teach you. First, the bacon grease is still hot, so you add some flour...not too much now, a small handful, and then grind in some pepper and salt and swoosh it around good till it's thick and smooth and the flour has soaked up all the grease. Now, hand me the coffeepot. See, I add it in and keep swooshing 'til it's smooth, and there you go."

Adelaide raised her hand. "Yes, Addie, what is it you want?"

"I would like butter too."

"You would, would you? Black gravy is good enough for your daddy and me, it's good enough for you,"

"Tommy, it appears we ain't getting no butter today."

"No, Lady, we ain't."

"Aren't." Serena said. "You all eat up. We got to get to church and I don't want to be the family that follows the choir in this time."

Amy had been staring at her grits and gravy for a while as if unsure what she was expected to do with them. In fairness, if you weren't raised on grits, if this were your first encounter with them and the gravy applied on them, you might have some second thoughts about how hungry you were. She dug in a spoon and popped a portion into her mouth. A trace of a smile flickered and she proceeded to clear her plate.

"Miss Serena, am I going to church with you?"

"It's Sunday, child. Where else would you be going in the morning?"

• ● ● ● •

As it turned out, they managed to be comfortably ensconced in a pew toward the back of the church when the choir processed and all stood to sing "Onward Christian Soldiers." Amy sang along with the rest of them, indicating to Jesse that she had some familiarity with the whole churching business. He still struggled with the Methodist way of doing things. He'd been raised a Primitive Baptist and the idea of spending only an hour or so at worship was a novelty, to say the least. Back on the mountain, church could be an all-day affair with preachers taking turns at alternately shaming the congregation and calling down hellfire and brimstone on a corrupt and sinful world. This Methodist preacher seemed more intent on gearing up the congregation for fairs, fêtes, suppers, and fundraisers.

Amy received a few looks from what Jesse referred to as "the Old Biddies." The fact she had a noticeable bump and no ring on her left hand meant she would be the topic of conversation over cups of tea in parlors across town the rest of the week. It didn't help that the sermon was on "The Wages of Sin." The blood drained from Amy's face. For a second, Jesse thought she might faint. She didn't. If she hadn't been boxed in by the rest of his brood, Jesse was sure she'd have bolted.

During the worst of it, he saw Serena pat Amy's hand. She seemed better after that.

• ● ● ● •

Jesse had them off to an early start up the Buffalo. Serena had packed a hamper of staples. Addie Sutherlin would not admit to it, or perhaps did not know, that she'd been forgetting things lately. Her mind seemed sharp enough most days, but lately things like names and occasional faces and. more importantly, her daily routines, had slipped a bit. That is, she had slippage in her sense of time and place. She'd make a pot of hot water because she'd forgotten to add the coffee to the mix, or she'd run out of flour or cornmeal. Sometimes she'd have the items, but had put them away in the wrong place. Serena's hamper contained enough things put up in mason jars and boxes to last a week or two. There was no guarantee that she'd use them. Serena had asked Jesse, near to insisting, but all appeals for Addie to move to town and live with them had been rejected, and not gracefully.

Jesse pulled up to the house. His mother sat on the porch, leaning forward in her rocker as if she couldn't be sure who had arrived.

"That you, Jesse?"

"Hey-do, Ma. Yep, it's me and Serena and the young'uns."

"Well, I declare. What're you all doing up here?"

"It's Sunday, Ma. We most always come up here on Sundays."

"No. It's Sunday already? Mercy, I must have missed church. Did I? Oh, well, Reverend Bob will come calling now, I reckon. Who's that with you?"

Amy walked around the car and helped Serena with the hamper. The four children scampered across the yard and up the porch steps.

"This here is Amy Cates. She's staying with us for a spell."

Amy and Serena lugged the wicker basket up to the house and carried it in. Addie gave Amy the once-over. Amy said later she felt like she had walked through one of them fluoroscope machines she read about where they could see you like you didn't have any clothes on.

"You spent some time 'rastling in the hayloft, seems like," Addie said.

"Ma'am?"

"You has got yourself in the family way, ain't you? Where's the boy who put you there?"

Amy started to tear up.

"That's a whole different story, Ma. Maybe for later."

"He's dead. Somebody stabbed him with a pitchfork, they said."

"Well, now, that's the way it is with men what preys on innocent girls, honey. Don't you cry. It's bad but not the end of the world. Is it, Serena?"

"No'm, it isn't. There is them that preys on girls and them, like us, that prays for girls. So, don't you fuss any more, girl. You got a whole life to live yet."

With that, Amy collapsed on the floor and sobbed as if her heart would break.

Chapter Eighteen

Addie stood and collected Amy in her arms. She rocked her for a few minutes. Amy calmed a bit, her sobs reduced to sniffles and hiccups.

"Jesse," Addie said, "do you remember Violet McAdoo?"

"Ma'am? I might. Seems a while back."

"Well, maybe you didn't. You weren't no bigger than a cricket back then, come to think of it."

"What about Violet McAdoo?" Serena asked.

"Well, just this. You listen careful, Sis," she said to Amy. "Seems like yesterday but it was in ought-four, I think. Whenever. This man drove his wagon out this way and stopped down the road not far from where your sawmill is at, Jesse, only it weren't the same mill back then, 'course. It were Abner Crouch's then, 'fore R.G. Anderson bought it. Well, anyway, like I said, he pulls up and puts down this girl, couldn't have been any older than you, Missy, and he hands down her little wicker case and says something like, 'You want to live like backward folk, you live with them here.' And, by gar, he drove off and left her standing in the middle of the road. She was sobbing just like you done, girl. Well, my pa, that'd be Big Tom McAddo to you, seen the whole thing. He goes up to her and right away he sees she's got herself in trouble like you done, Missy. So he packs her back to his house and gave her a place to stay. We all might be considered backward and short on the civilized way of doing things, but we don't throw folks on the compost pile either."

"Big Tom did that?"

"That's what I said, didn't I?" Addie paused and her eyes seemed to shift out of focus. After a moment she turned to the girl. "See, she moved in and had herself a very fine-looking baby, a boy. Well 'bout a year later Ross McAdoo come up on the mountain after trying his hand out west someplace. Oh, he was a sketch, Ross McAdoo was. Had some fine stories to tell. All about Indians and cowboys, just like you hear about. Well, sir, he wasn't here more'n a week or two and then one day he clapped eyes on Violet and took to her right away and next thing you know they is married and on their way to Danville and a new life. Now, ain't that something?"

"Yes'm, it is. But what has this to do with…?"

Addie fixed Amy with a look that preempted any response short of the truth. "Amy Cates, can you cook?"

"Some, yes'm. Miss Serena has taught me to make black gravy and grits."

Serena leaned in. "She can make a passable apple pie, Addie. And can fry up eggs and ham a treat."

"You can make gravy?"

"Yes'm"

"And be a fry cook?"

"Yes'm, I think so."

"Well, that settles it. I got me some old frocks that'll do 'til Jesse can fetch your poke up here. So, how about this? You come live with me. I ain't as sharp as I need to be, as either of my sons will tell you. I need some help with the remembering and chores, and they need to stop fussing about me and what might happen if I fell or wandered off and forgot where I was or maybe who I was, like Ella Parkins done. Poor soul. She was wandering around the woods no more'n a hundred yards from her house for almost two days 'fore they found her. Anyway, you'd be doing me a blessing and I can maybe help you through what comes next. Every girl who's going to birth a baby needs her ma. Yours is missing. I reckon I can fill in. How's that sound?"

"You'd take me in, even like I am?"

"That's pretty much it. You will be my Violet. We'll get you set up here on the mountain. Next thing we run you over to Granny Tidwell and find out what you got going on in that belly of yours. Once you drop your calf, who knows? Maybe your Ross McAdoo will drop by."

"Ma'am, you'd take me on? Just like that?"

"That's what I said, didn't I? Well, iffen you want, 'course, but yes."

"Can I ask another favor?"

"I don't know. How far do you think I should go?"

"My pa put me out. He said I wasn't no daughter of his and I was dead to him. So, if that is the case, I wonder if I could be a Sutherlin 'stead of a Cates."

"You want to be Amy Sutherlin?"

"Yes'm. You and Miss Serena and Jesse is the only decent folks I met in a long time. My family has cut me loose, so part of starting over ought to be joining up with folks who treat me like family."

"Well, now, if that don't cause no problem with the rest of the Sutherlins, I think we'd be right honored."

"Okay by me," Jesse said. "Abel won't have no problem either."

"Then it's done. Now tomorrow evening, Jesse, you run Amy's duds up here. Amy, you hop up and help me put our supper together."

Jesse and Serena had a long talk about Amy Cates on the drive home and whether her moving in with his mother was a blessing or a curse. The children were alternately sad and happy. They had come to like Amy during her short stay with them and allowed as how they'd miss her. On the other hand, acquiring a new aunt had a certain appeal, as well. On balance, Addie's amazing offer seemed to them to be for the best for both Amy and her.

"Did you ever hear about this Violet your ma talked about?"

"Can't honestly say, Serena. Like she said, it was back when I was maybe four, so, no. Why?"

"No reason, exactly. It's just something you don't run into often, is it? Who's that sitting on the porch? You haven't crossed another lawman, have you?"

Jack Braddock was parked on their front porch.

"That there is Captain Jack, if I ain't mistaken."

"That'd be the man who was in charge of you all during the war?"

"The very one. What in tarnation is he doing way out here on a Sunday evening?"

Jesse parked and unloaded the kids and the empty hampers. The children tumbled out of the car and gamboled toward the house, only to be brought up short by the image of a tall man with a moustache you'd expect to see on a general.

"Captain Braddock. This here is a surprise. What brings you all the way down from Washington, DC?"

"Howdy, Lieutenant. And it's Major now."

"Well, I'll be. Now that is something. Last I heard, all the officers was busted down to near nothing after we all got home."

"That was so. Then the few of us that stuck it out got a chance to move along, like our boss, McArthur. But we can talk about that later. I just wanted to stop by and let you know I'm in town and need to talk to you about Henry. I can't do it out at your work because it appears Henry works for you. How'd that come to be is a story I'd like to hear."

"Well, step in and I will tell you. Oh, sorry, this here is Serena, my wife, and these sprats is, in order, Tommy, Jake, LJ, and Lady, that's Adelaide actually."

"Well, you got yourself a fine-looking family there, Jesse. I won't bother you any more of the Sabbath, but tomorrow, if you have an hour or two to spare, I'd like to have some time together. I am staying at the hotel."

"Lunchtime tomorrow do?"

"Perfect."

"Any advance info I need?"

"Talk tomorrow."

Jack Braddock climbed down the steps, hopped into his Stutz, and drove off. Jesse tracked him down the road until he took the turn onto the main road.

"Well, that there is a mystery, for sure."

Chapter Nineteen

Floyd's best hotel, some would say its only hotel, but they discounted Martin's Stay-a-Night Cabins on the edge of town, had a decent lunchroom off the lobby. Lobby would be an overstatement, as well. Jesse spied Braddock alone at a table in the corner near a window. The view wasn't much, just the alley that led to the back loading dock and an array of garbage cans. Still, it did provide some sunlight and that had to count for something. Braddock stood when he caught sight of Jesse and waved him over. At the same time he signaled for Betty McGuire, the lunchroom's only waitress to take their order. Jesse and Betty arrived at the same moment.

Betty slouched over the table as the men seated themselves. "What'll you all have?

"Coffee and one of them Smithfield ham sandwiches. Put a little lettuce and a tomato slice in there with a dab of mayo, will you?" Jesse said.

"I'll have the same," Braddock said.

Betty sashayed to the portal that opened to the kitchen. "Two orders of Garden Smithies and two joes." Betty barked to any and all within hearing, presumably the folks in the kitchen.

Jesse and Braddock made small talk while they waited for their lunch. Jesse was wondering what had brought his old company commander down to this relatively remote part of the world from Washington, DC, but bided his time. Braddock would tell him when he was good and ready. Betty arrived with their lunch, refilled their water glasses, and swished off to attend to another table.

"So, our old general. What about McArthur?" Jesse said.

"You didn't know?"

"Know what?"

"He took on the Olympic team this summer. Managed it, coached it, even. They say he showed up in knickerbockers and a whistle and ran them boys ragged. He brought home twenty-eight medals, by God. That there is something to be proud of."

"Olympics? Sorry, they don't make much of a shadow down here."

"Right. This is the backcountry, I guess. Okay, so, Henry Sturgis is working for you, is that right?"

"He is, yes, sir."

"How come he came down here to Virginia? He was from up in Massachusetts, wasn't he?"

"So he says. I ain't sure what give him the itch, but he came here to scratch it. He showed up a couple of months ago. He said when he got home from France, he got a big welcome and such and he expected to be put to work right away. He has relatives, uncles and so on up there, who all have mills and shops. Job seemed pretty much a go. Anyway, he said not much worked out for him. He didn't say why. Being a war hero don't carry much water in peacetime. So, he says, he headed south. He remembered I was from down here somewhere and asked around. Next thing I know he's out at the mill and looking for work. He had some sawmill experience and he dropped right in. He's a good worker. Is there a special reason you want to know?"

"Maybe. So, how're you making out, Jesse? You got yourself married and a family."

"I do. How about you. Married?"

"Not yet. I am engaged, though, to a lady back in DC. Soon, maybe."

"It ain't none of my business, but how come when everybody else in the Army seems to be busted down to their permanent rank, you made Major?"

"Long story and for another day. Let's just say I have friends."

"Being a West Point boy didn't hurt none either, I reckon."

"No, it didn't. Did I say who my fiancée was?"

"Nope."

"Well, her father has a couple of stars on his shoulders, if you follow. Enough said. Okay, here's the thing about Henry. There is a board of review set up in the War Department. They are going over all the awards of the Meritorious Services Citation Certificate. Seems like too many soldiers with wounds in one foot or another were awarded it. The board's job is to sort out the ones who look like malingerers from the genuine and revoke their certificates and, maybe, take some action."

"Take action? They're going to court-martial them after all these years? How do they plan on doing that?"

"I don't think it's likely to come to that."

"This board of review, who all makes it up? Let me guess. Officers like full and light Colonels and such who've been busted back to Major. Like that?"

"Pretty much."

"Men who fought the war from farmhouses and soft billets a mile or two away from the trenches. Look, Captain—s orry, Major—I think that unless you spent some time in the mud, you got nothing to say about the who and what of the war. Henry was wounded. Period. Leave him be."

"Jesse, I got a job to do, so let me do it. I'm not here to mess with Henry. Just tell me how Henry got shot in the foot."

Jesse studied Braddock for a full minute. He liked this man. He trusted him. At the same time, he knew for a certainty that Braddock was a career Army man and would do what he deemed his duty, whether it hurt someone or not. He took a bite of his sandwich, sipped his coffee, and fiddled with his fork.

"Damnedest thing you ever saw. See, Henry was standing next to the parapet, if I recall right. He steps up. That was not a smart thing to do, 'course, but he did. Now, he had his head down, you know, like he's looking at his rifle which is in his hands, naturally, or maybe the ground to check his footing. I don't know. So, anyway, he rears up a mite and blam! Kraut sniper lets one loose. Well, the way his helmet is setting on his head, the bullet bounces off the dome part just short of where the brim starts, then it skips off the brim and the stock of his rifle. Did I say he was holding that piece like he was at Present Arms? No? Well, he were. So the bullet skips off the rifle butt and right into his foot. It were an amazing thing to see."

"Jesse…"

Jesse's eyes locked onto the Major's and held.

Jesse recalled the hours he'd spent in the trenches in France. Of the misery, the endless gnawing at your soul—would I be the next one to die? There wasn't a sane man there who at one time or another did not consider shooting themselves in the foot or holding up a hand in the hopes some show-off German sniper would shoot them and give them the "go home" wound. He hadn't, but he knew others had—a whole lot of doughboys sick and tired of the senseless killing, the idiotic orders from old men miles away, the whole sorry mess that war brings. No one, and certainly not Jesse, begrudged Henry his premature exit from the war.

"God's truth, Major Jack."

Braddock drummed his fingers on the tablecloth, swallowed the last of his coffee, and shook his head. Then, a decision made, he smiled a quirky smile and stood. "Okay, then. I'll report Henry's wound certifiable." He dropped two dollars on the table. "Gotta run, Jesse. Good talk."

He turned on his heel and disappeared through the door.

Jesse would not see him again for another five years.

Chapter Twenty

Jesse made it home in time for supper. Serena had a few things to say about that. "As rare as hen's teeth" popped up somewhere in her running commentary. Jesse nodded and listened. Love, he knew, came in funny-shaped packages and he wasn't in a mood to argue about this particular one.

"So what did the Captain and you chat about at lunch and how much did it cost you?"

"He's a Major now and it didn't cost me a thin dime, Serena, and Henry Sturgis was the topic of conversation, if you must know."

"The Captain paid? I mean the Major. He paid? Mercy. What financial miracle will we see next? What about Henry?"

"It was about how he came to get himself shot in the foot. So, how was your day?"

"My day? Well, funny you should ask. It's not something you ask me about most days."

"Serena…?"

"Jesse, it's just lately you been either out looking for a murderer who's probably dead and gone, that old watch, or everything else except us here at home. And these children are not getting more civilized, like I supposed they would once we got them off the mountain. I swear, they are like Indians on the warpath half the time."

Serena took a deep breath, sat, and fanned herself with her apron. "Never mind, I'm just in a state. It happens this time 'most every month. So, I went to the library, like I said I would. I got you a book on furniture-building, like you asked, and I got me a book 'bout economics."

"Eco…whats?"

"Economics. It's the study of how money is made and used, mostly. It says it's about goods and services, but, in the end, it's mostly 'bout money. It's by some foreigner named Nikolai Bukharin and it's called *Economic Theory of the Leisure Class.*"

"The leisure class? Well, that won't have nothing to say to us. Except for Sunday noontime, there ain't a whole lot of leisure to be had in this family."

"For sure. So, I was just browsing in it, you could say, trying to get a feel for the shape of it. I saw in the front index page that there was a whole chapter about 'Futures' so I thought that must be about what was going to happen. You know, Lawyer Bradford is so all-falluting crazy about getting rich, and the way them stock shares is going to grow forever. I figured I'd read up on it and find out what was coming."

"And?"

"It weren't about that at all. It was about commodity trading. Did you know that some of those big farmers out west sell their crop 'fore they even plant it?"

"What? How in Holy Ned do they manage that? Who's going to buy something that don't exist?"

"Traders. See, the farmer sells his crops in what they call a futures market. That way he has cash money to buy seed, machinery, and so on. The buyer is betting he can sell the crop after harvest at a higher price per bushel for…say, corn…than he paid for it in the spring."

"Now that there is a puzzle, for sure. People really do that?"

"Not just farmers. There's fruit growers, and all sorts of people who produce things that have prices that can change over time.

Just like the stock shares. You buy them at a price and reckon they'll be worth more later on. Isn't that what Mister Bradford said?"

"Yeah, well, what if there was a drought and the farmer couldn't deliver or the price per whatever fell below what the trader paid?"

"I reckon the farmer would have to go out and buy from other folks at the going rate to make up the shortage. In the second case, the trader loses his shirt."

"Lordy, what a world. Sometime I think we should have stayed up on the mountain. At least most of the time, what folks up there do makes sense. Anyway, I can't see where this has anything to do with us."

"Didn't you buy timber rights at a price with the notion you could sell them on to R.G. for more than you paid?"

"Well, yeah, but, that wasn't about waiting for a crop to come in. The trees was already there. Not much left hereabouts to speculate on now."

"You sure? I'm surprised you haven't noticed, but the timber that was cut forty-eight years ago has pretty much growed back. There's good pine and cedar. You run the only sawmill around. You might could think about getting back in the building trade business and buying up some timber rights now."

"Mill pine? I don't know, Serena. We're working full-out now with the hardwoods. They're our bread and butter. I don't know how we could add soft woods into the mix."

"All I'm saying is, maybe you should think about it."

"If I put anymore 'maybes' into my brain, I swear, it will explode."

● ● ● ● ●

Sheriff Privette waved Jesse back to his office. Jesse had stopped at the sheriff's office on the off chance something, anything, might have turned up.

"Back here, Jesse. I might have something for you."

Jesse worked his way between the clutter of the Sheriff's Department to the cubbyhole that served as Privette's desk. The sheriff pointed to a chair and Jesse sat. Privette spent another minute or two shuffling through the papers on his desk and finally looked up. Jesse thought he didn't look so good, like maybe the sheriffing business was a mite too strenuous for him. Privette coughed and blew his nose.

"Got me a cold. How, I can't imagine. I was out to the elementary school back a while. I reckon some runny nosed kid did me. Anyway, I got something for you, Jesse. I was poking around the various pawn shops and jewelry stores looking for that watch of yours, like I said I would."

Jesse was pretty sure he remembered the exact opposite, that Privette had no intention of trying to find it or anything else related to the murder, but held his tongue.

"There is a shop out the main drag that has one of those Jefferson Davis medals for sale. It might be from the chain of your watch. I don't know. You could check that out. Who knows, it might lead you back to the watch and maybe the killer, too."

"You're okay with me poking around a little? I thought you wanted me to leave the policing to you all."

"I do, but I ain't got time or men to spare to follow up on every little bitty piece of maybe evidence in a ten-year-old murder."

"Well, that is mighty fine of you, Sheriff."

Privette grunted and scribbled on a scrap of paper and handed it over the desk. Jesse fumbled for his reading glasses and perched them on his nose. He did not recognize the name or the address.

"Thank you, Sheriff. If this turns up anything, I'll be sure to let you know."

"You do that. I ain't holding my breath, you know."

"Gotcha."

Chapter Twenty-one

As much as Jesse wanted to go straight to the pawn shop and check out what the sheriff had discovered, he had a job and there was work to be done. He was already running late—again. Orders were piling up and the equipment he had to work with, while adequate to the task on an ordinary day, was now stretched to and beyond its capacity. He'd asked for more hours from the hands and they were happy to earn the extra pay, but the days were growing shorter and without floodlights or some method of lighting up the yard, that option was played out. Then there was the equipment. If even one of the saws were to go down, if one more blade had to be replaced, if one band saw coughed to a standstill, the mill would be in serious trouble. R.G. had to upgrade or he'd soon be out of business. R.G., of course, was in a place where none of that seemed to affect him. A new owner could fix that, but who and when?

●●●●●

The zing of saws ripping through wood and the smell of new sawdust greeted Jesse when he stepped from his car. He saw Henry Sturgis with a group of men inspecting the remains of a set of rails that had been taken out of service years ago. If Jesse remembered correctly, they were part of the original set-up. The dogs could probably be greased and put back into service. He wasn't so sure about the mandrel or the flat track. When rust reached a certain point, whatever it covered was pretty much done. The same could be said for the rack and pinion set.

Henry caught sight of him when he was six feet away.

"Look here, Jesse, Willie says give him a day or two and he could have this old set-up working again. If we can put another rip saw into operation, we could step up production and maybe get caught up. What do you reckon?"

"I got my doubts, Henry. That there rust looks like it might have eat clear through on parts of the arbor, and the rack and pinion looks as bad."

"Willie says when he was poking around in the toolshed, he found a bunch of parts wrapped up in oily rags that could be fitted to this set-up. Seems like at one time whoever was running this place had a mind to repair it and then forgot, or something."

"That's fine, if they can be used. The next question is, where we going to find a source to run the belt? Every tractor and steam engine we got is full-on right now."

Willie kicked at the rust and spat. "Well, Jesse, here's the t'ing. That big Allis you got over dere can run a second take off. I fit another pulley wheel on the side opposite of the first one and we set this up side-by-side wid the bigger rig and dere you go."

"Well, what the hell? It can't hurt to try. Then, when we get caught up, I got another idea how we can use this set of tracks. It was designed for a whole different kind of work, I think."

Jesse decided that come the weekend, he would get up in the mountains and secure some rights of first refusal on some pretty good tracts of loblolly pine. A passel of land owners who he knew by name were sitting on those tracts. He also knew they were disinclined to harvest the timber themselves. They'd dealt with him in the past and would again.

● ● ● ● ●

Manikin's Collectables, Est. 1920, turned out to be a small clapboard store that had seen better days. Jesse thought that if the owner really wanted to improve his business, he's spruce the place up a bit.

He pushed through the door and a bell attached to the jamb tinkled him in. The proprietor, Manikin himself, as it turned out, greeted him. Jesse noticed he had a .38-caliber police special strapped to his hip. Manikin's Collectables apparently catered to a slightly different clientele than its name implied. Manikin was a big, burly man with a beer belly and what Jesse guessed were permanent sweat stains under his arms. Still, there was a steely quality about how his eyes focused on you. Jesse reckoned this was a man he'd as soon not tussle with.

"Yes, sir, what can I do for you?" Manikin asked.

"You have a Jefferson Davis Guard medal, they tell me. I'd like to see it, if I could."

"You a collector? Because if you are, I have a whole section devoted to Civil War, sorry, you all call it something else—"

"We call it that, too. No, I ain't looking to buy me anything like that. I have an interest in a Davis Guard medal, mostly."

"Okay." Manikin reached for a drawer behind him, pushed the items in it around with a forefinger that more nearly resembled a sausage, and retrieved the medal. "It's a beaut, ain't it? You don't hardly see these. Some fella said they was rare."

"They are. They were only awarded to soldiers who did some pretty amazing things in battle. It was like the Congressional Medal of Honor the North gave out. Only they ended up being almost like Cracker Jack prizes in the end."

"That so? Well, here you go. Have a look. I'll make you a good price."

Jesse turned the medal to inspect its back. "Nope, this ain't the one."

"Ain't the one what?"

"I'm looking for a particular medal. It was given to my grand-daddy. It had his initials 'graved on the back. Like you said, they're rare and so I figured there'd be a chance this one was his. But it ain't."

"Well, I'm mighty sorry about that. How'd you come to lose it in the first place?"

"Me? No, I didn't lose it. It were attached to my pa's watch chain and that were stolen from him couple of years back by the man who robbed and killed him."

"That a fact? Well, I'll be. This watch and chain. What'd it look like?"

"It was a big gold watch. We kids called it the Onion 'cause it was so big and fat. It had a case that flipped open and his initials was 'graved inside that, too."

"You say it was stole?"

"Yep. Well, thank you for your time. I reckon I'll have to keep looking."

"Hold on a minute. Let me think. When was this watch stole?"

"Near to ten years ago, why?"

"A while back a man did come in here looking to sell me a watch just like that and, by Godfrey, it had a medal like this one on the chain, like you said."

"Who was it?"

"I can't rightly say. See, I just moved down here from Fredericksburg about then. Opened up this shop and he must have been an early customer. I offered him five dollars. He needed twenty. I said ten was my best offer and he left mad. Never saw him again."

Jesse could barely hide his excitement. This could be the lead he needed. "What was his name?"

"No idea. Like I said, I was brand new to town and 'fore you ask, I don't keep records on 'no sales.' I can tell you he was a big man and pushy, you know? Like he thought he was important or in charge. Didn't impress me none. Anyway, he tosses me a cuss and leaves."

Jesse's hopes dropped into his shoes. He was so close, and

then nothing. "Thanks, anyway. Say, listen, if he comes back or that watch turns up again, will you let me know?" He pulled a sheet from his notebook and scribbled his name and the phone number at the sawmill on it and slid it across the counter.

"You work out at the lumber yard?"

"It's a mill, mostly and the lumber we have is mostly already sold. The mercantile keeps some building supplies out back, if that's what you're after."

"I am, but they ain't got much to show. I need a lot to straighten this shop out and build me a storeroom on the back."

"Maybe by spring, we could oblige you."

Jesse left, disappointed. What to do now? Who was the man with the watch?

Chapter Twenty-two

Jesse did not head straight home after work. Instead, he made a detour toward the mountains. Serena would soon understand if he was late for supper. His route took him up into familiar ground. Too familiar, he guessed. He'd been looking at the forests all his life. Trees grew, but slowly. Unless you made an effort, you didn't notice how much. Now, he took notice. Serena was right. The acreage that had its timber harvested in the nineties and even earlier, had grown back. Loblolly pine, he knew, grew fast. Some of the trees stood nearly ninety feet tall and were more than ready to be harvested again. Since the area had been clear-cut and back then, there'd been no real effort or intention to reseed or replant, he reckoned it a near miracle that the timber had made such an impressive comeback. Serena was onto something. Come the weekend, he'd make another foray up in the mountains and do something about "trading in futures," only this crop was ready to harvest right now.

He spent an hour walking the slope of the Buffalo measuring the timber by eye and guessing the sellable board feet each might produce. He thought he heard an automobile down on the road near where he'd parked, but couldn't be sure.

What he was sure he heard was the bolt action of an Lee-Enfield rifle.

He dropped to the ground. A sliver of bark from the tree next to him flew away at the same time he heard the report. Jesse had no time to think. Someone was shooting at him and it surely was the same person who'd shot Elroy. How many Lee-Enfield rifles could there be?

Then he remembered Manikin the pawnbroker. There could be several.

He waited four heartbeats and rose to his feet and stepped off in one smooth, simultaneous motion. He dodged between the trees and zigzagged his way down the hill toward his car.

Two, three, four. He counted the reports. Assuming the shooter had one in the breech and five in the clip, he needed to hear two more before he could run in a straight line while whoever was up there shooting at him reloaded. Five, six.

Jesse bolted straight downhill to his car and managed to get it started and rolling when the next shot punched a hole in the safety glass in the right rear window. Another put a hole in the roof. He pressed the accelerator to the floorboards as hard as he could. The old Piedmont sedan had not been designed for the race circuit, but on this rutted dirt road, it practically flew. Jesse had a momentary thought of finishing what the shooter could not by rolling the car off the road and down the hillside.

He didn't take the time to check out the car parked a quarter mile down the road. If it had a license plate he might have been able to trace its owner. On the other hand, if he stopped, he might be dead.

The next time he went up to look at trees, he would be carrying.

• ● ● ● ●

When he reported the shooting, Privette had been impressed at the damage to the car. He shook his head when he saw the bullet holes. "Whoo-ee, that was a close one. You say he was shooting a Lee-Enfield? How'd you know that?"

"I spent some quality time in the French mud listening to them being fired. Ask anybody who was there. It ain't something you forget."

"But you have no idea who might have been taking potshots at you?"

"Nope. I reckon it is somebody who is worried about me asking around about my pa's murder. I went to see that pawn-broker you found. Maybe he tipped off the shooter. He said there was a man—"

"Jesse, you sound like you been at the moonshine a mite too hard. Ain't it more likely that wandering around on the slope of the Buffalo like that, you came too close to somebody's still? You know how this is these days. Federal men busting up stills, folks shooting. It's dangerous up there. I think you just crossed paths with a moonshiner with an itchy trigger finger."

"Sheriff, that don't make any sense at all. First, everybody on the mountain knows me and knows I ain't about to rat them out to the government. Second, nobody sets up a still on a slope and in the open like that. You need to be near a source of water and cover. An open forest like that for a still? No way."

"If you say so, Jesse. You'd know all about that, I guess. All I'm saying is what's the likelihood that after all this time anybody is interested in a ten-year-old murder where there ain't no clues?"

"I got me a busted window and a bullet hole in my car's roof that says sure'n hell there must be."

There would be no convincing the sheriff. He'd closed his mind on finding a killer. Maybe he'd help recover the watch, which by now could have changed hands a dozen times, but solve the murder? Not going to happen.

Jesse parked the car around the back of the house. There was no sense in getting Serena all riled up. Somehow, Jesse needed to get the car's window repaired before Sunday. The bullet hole in the roof he thought he could cover up with a dab of putty and paint. Who had the parts to repair a window of a nineteen-twenty

Piedmont sedan? Did they even still make them? He'd have to check at Mort's garage and fuel stop.

Jesse climbed the steps to the kitchen door and pushed his way in.

"Jesse," Serena said, "what happened?"

"I'm not that late, am I?"

"No. What have you been up to?"

"Up to? What do you mean?"

"Jess, I have known you all my life. We have been married for eight years. There isn't anything about you I can't see. You have been in a scrape. I'm right, aren't I? What happened? You look awful."

"Well, thank you kindly for that compliment. You're looking fine your own self."

"Stop it, Jess. This isn't funny. What happened?"

Jesse considered his choices and decided that under the circumstances, a lie would serve him better than the truth. Besides, maybe the sheriff had it right after all.

"I was up on the Buffalo checking out the timber, like you said. I guess I must have stirred up someone sitting on a still, 'cause the next thing I know, someone is taking potshots at me. I hightailed out of there quick as I could, but one of the bullets must have strayed a mite and put a hole in the car's window."

Serena studied Jesse's face the whole time he spun his story. She sighed. "Okay, you aren't going to tell me what happened right now, I can see that. I just wish you'd remember we are married and we face things together. If someone wants you dead, Jesse, I need to know who and why. Go wash up for supper."

There were some clear drawbacks to being married to a smart woman, he knew. So, how much should he tell her?

Chapter Twenty-three

Serena didn't have much to say during supper or the following morning at breakfast, either. You didn't need a special delivery letter to know when she had a mad on. It wasn't so much a matter of Jesse wanting to keep her in the dark as to not alarm her. Being shot at up on the Buffalo was not as rare as people might think and he had no proof beyond his gut that someone wanted him dead. Also, if he told her what he'd been up to prior to the shooting, told her about Manikin and the watch, she'd for sure turn down the temperature even more. All he could think to do was to push on and hope he'd come up with a solution before things got out of hand and someone, make that him, got bad hurt. He said his good-byes and headed over to Mort's Garage. He needed to get the evidence of his near-killing removed from the car as quickly as he could. If anyone could patch up the old Piedmont, it was Mort.

"You still driving that old clunker, Jesse? I'da thought you'da got yourself something more reliable by now."

"It's paid for, Mort, and that makes it a very fine automobile. I do have a small problem with it, though."

"Besides the fact that they ain't made one of these since twenty-two, what's the problem?"

"I was up on the mountain yesterday and someone took a notion to shoot at me. Well, maybe just the car. You can't ever know up there. So, anyway, I need me a new window in the back, like you can see, and there's a hole in the roof could use a patch."

Mort tapped the window that sported the bullet hole, snorted, and stood on his tiptoes to survey the car's roof. "You are in luck, my friend. This car is pretty much worthless on any day of the week, but parts to fix it are easy to come by. Piedmont went out of business in twenty-two but left a quarter of a million simoleons in parts behind. Me? I scooped up as many as I could afford. If you ain't noticed, most of the twenties cars is pretty much alike and the parts is interchangeable, or nearly so. You reposition a bolt hole here or a snap there, or maybe shave a quarter inch off this or that, and you have a part that can fix anything from a Lexington to a Moon, and I bet you ain't heard of neither." Jesse hadn't. "I can have that window replaced in a couple of hours and a little glue, fabric, and paint and that hole in the roof will disappear, too. So, you want to leave it?"

"Can you drop me off at the mill?"

"Sure. We'll drive your car and I'll see what else I can find to repair for you."

• ● ● ● •

Mort dropped Jesse off at the sawmill, tooted the horn, and chuffed away. The first thing Jesse noticed was the noise. There wasn't any. Only a single saw whined its way through a bole of an ancient oak. Men not working that rig stood around in groups smoking and chatting. Some had opened their lunch boxes and were sipping coffee. Jesse headed for the office.

"R.G., what in billy blue blazes is happening out there?"

R.G. looked up from his magazine and waved the stub of his cigar in greeting. "Happening out there? Not much, it looks like."

"Where's Henry? What's going on?"

"Oh, well, Henry said he had to go home for a day or two. He's off to Massachusetts or wherever he came from. He'll be back."

"Went home? When did he decide to do that? He didn't say by-damn nothing to me yesterday."

"Can't say, Jesse. I saw him in here later after work jawing on the telephone with a pile of orders in front of him. The ones that cancelled this morning, by the way, and then he says he has to get on home and he'll be back toot sweet. I suppose the men ain't so sure about what to do because we had orders cancelled."

"What orders been cancelled?"

"All them in that pile there."

Jesse rifled through the pile of papers on his desk. "We got no orders?"

"Oh, we got work, just a whole lot less than we did yesterday, is all."

"What happened?"

R.G. picked up the magazine he'd been reading. "It's all in here. Seems the furniture business has outrun its market. They figured that with the economy booming, folks would be buying new every year or so. Seems like they was wrong. Look here. There's ads put in here by the makers asking for salesmen to take on their line and there's ads by salesmen looking for lines to take on. Furniture ain't moving and they're betting if they get more folks out to selling or if the salesmen has more things to sell, they can turn it around. Probably wishful thinking. Folks don't see the need to replace furniture like they do cars or dresses and such."

"You're saying there is a slump in the furniture market?"

"Maybe. I think it's more like the market is overstocked. Sales is steady but there's too much inventory. Look, think about it for a minute. All this boom in the economy. Who's really getting rich? The average man in small-town America ain't got no part in it, really, beyond he's got a paycheck and maybe some money in the bank. City folk with money to invest, now they might be buying furniture every whipstitch, but not you or me. A boom here or there don't mean a boom everywhere, see?"

"Okay, I see that, but why are all the men standing around? We still have orders to fill and there is raw stock out there that can be cut to standard lengths and got ready for the future."

"There you go. You hop on out there and get them working. You know, I just hope to sell this whole operation off and get me a piece of quiet 'fore I die. You thought about it, Jesse, buying me out? You, of all the people I know, are the most likely to keep this place going."

"I thought about it, R.G., but I ain't come to a conclusion yet."

"Won't be on the table forever."

Jesse went out into the yard and put the men to work reducing the stock trees to standard widths and lengths. There was enough work to keep them busy for at least another month. After that, if the furniture business continued to dry up, he reckoned they could get on with soft woods cut for the building trade.

Saturday was market day. Saturday folks came into town to shop and socialize. Saturday, Jesse would start collecting the timber rights to all that new yellow pine growing up in the mountains. Furniture might be lagging, but folks still needed houses, farmers need barns and sheds, and if a new house wasn't in the books, well a small house could get added onto. Pawnbrokers needed more rooms and the shelving to go in them. Anderson's mill was about to go back to its roots and mill two-by-fours, two-by-sixes, four-by-eights and in eight- and twelve- foot lengths, and Jesse was going to provide the timber. He'd stop by Lawyer Bradford on his way home and pick up some ready-made contracts.

"Hey, Jesse?" R.G. was waving him over to the office.

"What's up, R.G.?"

"I swear I feel like your personal telephone operator. You got another phone call, man wants to see you."

"Who was it?" Jesse said when it looked like R.G. wasn't going to say any more.

"Eh? That junk dealer fella. Michigan?"

"Manikin?"

"The very fella. He wants to see you, soon's you could make it into town."

Chapter Twenty-four

Mort had returned Jesse's car fixed near as dammit like-new before lunch so Jesse drove into town and pulled up in front of Manikin's shop. The door to the store stood ajar and the screen door slapped against the jamb as a gust of October wind hit it. It wasn't exactly cold out, but it wasn't springtime either.

Jesse stepped into the street and walked toward the shop. He couldn't be sure, but he thought he heard a door slam shut in the distance, maybe out back. He pushed into the store. There was no sign of Manikin.

"Mister Manikin? You here?"

No answer. Jesse walked around the counters and made his way to the back. Manikin had a room in back where he kept his books and inventory. Manikin himself lay next to his desk bleeding from a nasty gash in his side. Jesse knelt, checked the wound and the blood pouring from it and knew Manikin had only seconds to live. Jesse had seen men gutted by a bayonet before. Many times. Too many times.

Manikin coughed, moaned, and rolled his eyes. He caught sight of Jesse and let out a sigh.

Jesse leaned in. "Who done this?"

"He came back. I was going to tell you…I remem…"

"Who came back?"

"Man with…watch. I 'member'd he was in earli…er 'n bought an Enf…"

"The man who wanted to sell you the Onion bought an Lee-Enfield? When?"

"Two, three…week. He came back and asked about you and then…"

"And then?"

Manikin was done talking. Jesse found the phone beside the desk where it had been knocked off and called the sheriff's office.

● ● ● ● ●

Sheriff Privette's men cleared the crime scene in what Jesse thought was pretty much a hurry. Privette took his statement and scowled at the idea that this murder had anything to do with the murder of Jesse's father. Jesse wondered if the sheriff was just naturally thick, slow to pick up on the obvious, or, and this was the scary part, complicit in either or both. He refrained from mentioning the last but did suggest the first two in passing. Privette was not pleased.

"Exactly what were you doing in here, Jesse?"

"Doing? I had a message from Manikin here, that he had something to tell me about the man who tried to sell him the Onion. He said—"

"That watch? How'd he know that one was your granddaddy's watch?"

"He didn't, exactly. I described the watch and the Guards medal it had as a fob and he—"

"He didn't have no more idea it was the one you've been looking for than a chicken has teeth. You put that idea in his head and look what it got him."

"How can you say that? Listen, you were the one sent me to him in the first place. You said he had a Jefferson Davis Guard medal. I looked at the one he had and it weren't the one I'm after. Then he said he'd seen another one like it a bunch of years back on a watch chain some local slicker wanted to sell him. I described the Onion and he allowed as how it mighta been the one. That's it. Next thing I know, he sends for me and I find him here dying of a bayoneting."

"That's it?"

"No, it ain't. He also said he recalled selling that same man a Lee-Enfield rifle two or three weeks ago. Don't that make it for you? I been shot at multiple times by a Lee-Enfield. I been asking around about an item that could maybe link to the man who killed my pa. It's one plus one, Sheriff. You can add good as me."

"That ain't my 'rithmetic, son. Like I keep telling you. Policing is the business of the sheriff's office. You stand down."

"If this is the best you can do, I ain't standing down. You're about to let this slide away."

"I warned you, Jesse. Now listen close. As far as I can make it out the onlyist person who knows anything about bayoneting someone is standing right there in your shoes. Do you want me to run you in on suspicion of murder?"

"You're having me on. You plan on charging me with killing this man. Why would I do that?"

"Oh, I could come up with something if I put my mind to it. Besides, it don't matter a lick one way or the other. I just want you to butt out. Got it?"

Jesse could feel the blood rising up his neck and across his face. He stared at the sheriff in disbelief. There was something else going on here besides mule-headedness. Privette had a flea in his ear and it was wreaking havoc with more than just him. Jesse took a breath and headed toward the door.

"You want to put me in the hoosegow, you know where to find me."

● ● ● ● ●

Serena had thawed out a bit since breakfast. What Jesse had to tell her would for sure, put her back into something like the North

Pole. That was a chance he'd have to take. It was time she knew. He sent the kids into the backyard to play and sat Serena down at the kitchen table. He talked for a half hour without pausing. Serena listened without interrupting even once. Her expression shifted from angry, to annoyed, to frightened, to fierce. The last Jesse took as a good sign. When Serena took it into her head to fight about something, the battle was as good as won.

When he finally stopped, with one last apology for not listening to her, she sat perfectly still, her face impassive. The clock on the parlor struck seven. The children had fled from the growing darkness and were huddled on the back porch like puppies waiting to be let in. Somehow they knew that their parents were at a place where they needed to be quiet as mice. Four pair of eyes stared in through the screen door's mesh. The clock stopped chiming and resumed tick-tocking.

Serena signaled for them to come in. Without a word they trooped in.

"Ya'll get ready for bed. Your daddy and me need to have a word and then we'll be up to tuck. Now git."

When they'd cleared the room, Serena stared off into space for what seemed to Jesse an eternity. Finally, she turned to him. "We're a pair, Jess. I don't know what drives you to all the time wanting to do the right thing, but it was one reason I'm sitting here and we got us a family and a house. We go together, you and me, like night and day."

"Like thunder and lightning, you mean."

"Let me finish. This is serious. It's been that way ever since that night up on the Buffalo when we first knew each other. It doesn't end because we're in a scrape. So here's what we do. It seems pretty clear the sheriff has got petrifaction of the brain. So, you and me are going to have to figure this out instead. I have one thing I need from you."

"What's that?"

"You stop trying to protect me from everything. I can't hardly help if you're fibbing about things. You were shot at, not once but twice, by someone who is certain he wants you dead. If we don't catch him soon, he'll succeed and I do not have any plans ready on becoming a widow.

"So, here's what we do. First, you start packing that pistol of yours all the time. Second, you get a friend to walk with you. Bring him in on the situation, someone you can trust. Four eyes are always better than two. Also, we might should consider moving back up on the mountain. We'd be safe there. Any stranger slipping through the woods up there is likely to end up in a crick with some holes in him he weren't born with."

"Serena, we can't just move. There's the chilun's school and—"

"I know all that. I said, 'consider,' as a last resort. In the meantime, you let me ask around. You'd be surprised what women talk about when they don't think menfolk are listening."

"You be careful. If whoever this is finds out you're poking around—"

"I know it. There's another thing. Not about the man who's after you. If I read right what R.G. is saying, there's more to those cancelled orders than he's letting on. Something about this 'Let's all get us rich boom' isn't right, somehow."

"So what do we do?"

"Let's get the rights to the timber up on the mountains locked up as soon as we can."

Chapter Twenty-five

On Friday, Serena told Jesse she needed to stop by the bank and would come home as soon as she'd finished. She left at eight sharp so as to be at the bank when it opened its doors.

He was a little taken aback when she didn't return until after nine. "Where you been? I thought you was to the bank and then straight back here?"

"I was, and here I am. I got caught up in a conversation with the teller and he couldn't answer my question, so he called the manager, and he didn't know either. Finally, I managed to track down Mister Babcock, the president, and he knew. He didn't want to share at first. He said it wasn't a woman's place, but he did finally."

"Did what?"

"Tell me what their discount rate was."

"The disc…the what?"

"We need to have a talk about our money in the bank, Jess, but not now. Looky here, I have a fist full of five- and ten-dollar bills. We are ready to do business."

"What are we going to do with all that money? I thought we were going to market day tomorrow to get folks to agree to give us first rights to their timber."

"We are. This is earnest money."

"What kind of money? Earnest?"

"When they sign, we give them a five-dollar or a ten-dollar pre-payment. That way they will know we are serious. Also, we let them know that if we don't exercise the option, they get to keep the money."

"Serena, a handshake and my word has always been fine and dandy up on the mountains. Them folks know I wouldn't ever stiff them. We don't need it."

"Do you really think you are the only person who has figured out that the hills need a haircut? Do you think you are the only one out here looking to pick up the rights?"

"You've heard something?"

"Like I told you, women talk. Now look. We are the ones they will come to as soon as they hear about the money. And then there is the other thing."

"What other thing?"

"Jesse, most of them come to town on market day to buy necessities. A bag of salt, a pound of sugar, maybe. Most will settle for molasses, and such, but they're here to get the basics. Most of them don't have much in cash money, and they will scrimp and even go halves with a neighbor to get what they need. When they understand that the five or ten dollars we give them is forever theirs, well, what do you think? They are going to remember Jesse Sutherlin, who was the one that gave them the best market day they ever had. There's needles and fabric or maybe a new poke that they'll get that wasn't anywhere near to being on their list, and they will remember you."

"You're sure about this?"

"It's time we moved into the world of business. Times have changed. You can still get by on a handshake here and there, but not everybody is so set on that way of doing things as before. There's them that will forget that handshake in a minute if they get leaned on or figure there's a better deal to be had. You know what the man said. 'Money talks.'"

"What man said that?"

"I don't know, but he did. Now let's get to work. Small acreage gets five dollars as soon as they sign. Big acreage gets ten. And no more! Don't you get all soft in the head if one of them tells you a sad story."

"I won't. Hey, where did you come up with all this, anyway?"

"I read books, Jess. I read and I learn. That's why I asked about the bank's discount rate. There's things you need to know if you don't want to be in the poor house or back on the mountain sharing your porch with the pigs."

● ● ● ● ●

Market day Saturday—the one day in the month when mountain folk and townspeople were likely to mix and mingle. It would be a misapprehension to assume the mixing carried with it a sense of community or even cordiality. They bartered, traded, bought, and sold, and when they were done, went home. The few words exchanged were connected to the transactions, not any effort to connect or socialize. At the same time, there would be no confrontations or angry words. A fight was rare, and if it occurred, would be fueled by moonshine, like as not.

By three in the afternoon, Jesse had corralled almost all of the good timber in the area. There were a few more tracts he'd like to have, but the owners did not show. Tomorrow was Sunday and there were laws about doing business on that day. That said, Jesse also knew that the law stopped where the mountain sloped up and the trees began. He reckoned after church he'd take another trip. First, however, he'd need the friend Serene insisted on, the sidekick, someone to watch his back. He'd agreed, if only to keep her happy. Hell, he got through a whole war. Why'd he need a nursemaid now?

Serena had collected the children from the playground and gone home. Jesse lingered, hoping he might land one more client.

"So, Jesse, here we are." William Kick held out his hand. Jesse shook it and looked the mechanic hard in the eye.

"Willie, this is going to sound odd, but do you happen to own a gun?"

"Me? Is there a law? What should I say?"

"I ain't concerned about no law. I need to know if you own one. If you do, I have a proposition for you."

"Okay, then, I do. It is German Luger I bring home from the war. Only just now I find ammunition for it, though."

"Really? Where'd you find it?"

"You know that place where the man was stabbed? Terrible thing, it was. So, I hear he has things like that for sale and I go there and buy what he has. It was lucky I find him when I did, yes?"

"When was that?"

"Now dat's funny. Now I think of it, it was the day he is killed."

"Think a minute, Willie. Was there anybody else in the store then?"

"Just some man in a worn-out suit that don't fit so good anymore. The west was not able to be buttoned and the knees was out. He was looking at…oh, mine Gott. He was with the rifles and the—"

"Bayonets?"

"Ja. You think he is the killer?"

"Probably. So, that's why I asked you about the gun." Jesse explained his situation, Serena's insistence he have a trusted friend with him and would he, Willie, be willing to be that person? Willie said that Jesse saved him from a life as a bum, gave him a job and respectability, so, yes, he would be happy to be Jesse's "Fuzzy."

"Be my Fuzzy?"

"You know, Tom Mix has this funny man who helps him in the moving pictures, yes?"

"If you say so. I don't get to the pictures much. Fuzzy, huh? Well, okay then. Tomorrow after church, you and me are heading up the mountain for an hour or so. Is that alright with you?"

"Sure."

"I got to git. I'll meet you at the sawmill at one, okay? And you can fill me in on the man in the shop."

"Maybe I should tell the sheriff?"

"Don't bother. He ain't interested."

Chapter Twenty-six

Jesse left the house as soon as he'd wolfed down his dinner. Serena was not pleased. He assured her he'd be back in time to make the Sunday pilgrimage up to Addie's on time and, yes, he had a friend to go with him and, yes, both he and the friend would be armed. It might be the last chance, or at least the best chance, to collect the few remaining timber rights that had any real value. Serena had to concede. After all, it had been her idea to go after them in the first place.

"Well, you go, then. Do I know this friend you'll be taking with you?"

"You've heard me talk about him. It's Willie Kick. He's a veteran, like me. I trust him."

"Okay, then. By the way, I aim to pull all our money out of the bank."

"What?"

"It isn't safe there, Jesse. The bank is stretched to the limit with loans. Mercy, it's in worse shape than R.G. Anderson's mill. If there was a run on the bank, they'd collapse."

"I don't understand. They have money, they loan it out. It comes back."

"I'll explain when you get back."

"Is this about the disc…whatever…thing?"

"Discount rate, yes. It's all in that economics books I been reading. Now, go. We'll talk later."

• ● ● ● •

The car with its new Carter carburetor hummed along like new. Actually, Jesse bought the car from R.G., who'd owned it for eight years before he sold it to Jesse, so he'd no real idea what it might have sounded like when new, but it ran pretty good and that was enough.

Willie waited for him at the mill gates. He climbed in and they headed out to the mountains. Jesse knew most of the folk he wanted to deal with. The few strangers, he'd tackle last. In the meantime, he wanted to pump Willie about the man in the store the day Manikin was killed.

Before he could start, Willie turned in the seat and asked, "Why won't the sheriff be interested in what I remember about the man who might have been the killer of the shopkeeper?"

A very good question. Jesse struggled for an answer. "Okay, here's what I meant. I been tracking down the man who mighta killed my pa back a decade. You know all about that. That's howcome we met, right? Every time I bring something to the sheriff about that, he drops it like a hot potato. I don't know why. I found Manikin's body…that's the man who owned the store, and called the sheriff right off. See, I was in that store a few days before, asking questions about a watch and Manikin had a few things to say. He remembered a man in a fancy suit who wanted to sell it. The way he described the watch, I was sure it were the Onion.

"Well, anyway, he called me and said he remembered something else and I should drop by. I get there and he's dead. I say to the sheriff, there has to be a connection between the watch and me being shot at the day before, and Manikin's being dead, and he says…well never mind what he said. He practically accused me of stabbing Manikin my own self. So that's why. I am probably wrong, Willie. When you get a chance, you should slip over to the sheriff's office and tell him what you know. Maybe then he'll take me seriously. Probably not, but you never know. So, tell me about the man. What do you remember?"

"Well, he was a big man, you know. I mean he was one time probably pretty fit. Fat but fit, if you follow. That suit I tell you about? It was one time very good. Cost a lot."

"How'd you figure that?"

"He flipped the lapel back to get a pencil, maybe, from the inside pocket and I see a label. Not what we see in store suit, but one that says something like 'Tailored for so and so by such and such" Like that."

"You saw the label?"

"Sure."

"What was the name?"

"It was not easy for me to read. It is gold thread worn out with many years of dirty hands on it. I make out tailor's name a little."

"Who?"

"All I see is Samuel."

"Samuel? That's all?"

"Sorry, yes."

"Well, it's a start. All I have to do is find me a tailor named Sam. This is our turn."

Jesse wheeled off the road and downshifted to take the grade. They climbed up the mountainside for five or six minutes. Then he pulled off the road and parked. The cabin he wanted to visit was a stiff climb up from there. He sat a minute staring at the rearview mirror.

"What're you waiting for, Jesse?"

"I'm checking to see if we picked up any company. The last time I came out this way, I was followed and damn near got killed. Twist around and check back along the road. You see anything?"

"Nah."

"Okay, you sit here and keep your eyes peeled back that way, while I go up the hill and have a chat with Enos Sanders about his timber."

Jesse started up the hill. Willie stepped out of the car and stood in the middle of the road. Another car came around the corner and stopped. Willie pulled his Lugar from his belt and made a show of checking its action. The car reversed, made a three-point turn, and drove away.

"Good work, there, Willie. You just scared the pants off Reverend Holloway."

"Who?"

"Baptist preacher from over in the next county."

"Would he want you dead?"

"It's possible. No way of telling now."

Jesse invited Willie to join them on the mountain at Addie's. For some reason, his mother did not raise a fuss about him bringing strangers for supper. Addie had a sixth sense about people, people said, and it was clear she took a shine to Willie Kick.

"So, you just plop yourself down here, Mister Kick. Amy, run get Mister Kick a iced tea. You like iced tea, Mister Kick? 'Course you do. Get a move on, Amy, the man is like to perish."

"Really, there's no need to—"

"Don't waste your breath, Willie. Count your blessings. Most strangers get the sharp edge of her tongue. You must have some German magic about you."

Amy scurried over with a glass of tea and stood back with her hands folded in front so as to minimize her growing middle. Willie took the glass and drank and smiled at both Addie and Amy.

"Mighty good tea you have here, Missus."

"Oh, I ain't no missus," Amy said.

"Is true? Well, that will be very good news for some lucky fella, sure."

Amy blushed and turned away. Addie squinted at Willie for a second and smiled.

"Ross McAdoo all over again, I swan," she muttered.

Only Jesse caught it. He shook his head. No matter how old and decrepit women might get to be, they never let go of romantic fancies, now did they? Willie and Amy as Ross and Violet. Really?

Chapter Twenty-seven

Addie set Amy and the older children to clearing the table and washing up. The younger ones were sent out to play in the pine needles while the light held and under the watchful eye of Serena and Nancy. The grownups sat on the porch, Addie in her rocker, and the others, Willie, Jesse, and Abel on whatever they could find. A moment later, Lady burst into tears because the boys were teasing her. Serena scooped her up and she joined the others on the porch, Lady in her lap.

"Why for do you call that child 'Lady,' Jesse? Her name is the same as mine. Ain't nobody ever called me Lady."

"Do you want to, maybe, rearrange that question, Ma?"

"What?"

"Never mind. Little Jess started it. He couldn't get his tongue around Adelaide and it come out Lady, so I guess you could say it stuck."

"Um. So how's it going with finding who it was killed your pa?"

Jesse ticked off the progress he'd made, the reluctance of the sheriff to take any of it seriously, and the danger it had put him—and, perhaps, the rest of them—in, and the reason Willie Kick was with them today.

"They come around me and mine and they will go home in a box," Abel said. "Whyn't you ask me to watch your back, Jesse?"

"First, you got a family to see to. Second, you're up here on the mountain and I ain't, so that's why."

"Well I coulda…"

"I know Abel, I know. I might need you later, so you stay ready. Okay, to answer your question, Ma, we have a few things to work with. There's the man who tried to sell the Onion. He's probably the same one who's following me. Willie, here, is with me so's to knock off any ideas he might have about catching me alone and unaware. 'Fore you ask, Abel, we can rule out any LeBruns. The man is a flatlander and Floyd local. That is why you all are safe up here. Ain't no flatlander with any sense coming onto Buffalo Mountain except with a posse. And maybe an armored car."

"Push gets to shove, we might be coming back and living in our house up mountain," Serena added. "We'd be pretty safe there."

"What I don't understand," Addie said," is why the sheriff is being so mule-headed about this."

"It's a puzzle, for sure. First, he wants me to lay back and leave the investigating to him, only he says ain't no point in doing any. Then he does nothing. Next, he tells me about a man who might help, but won't accept that what I'm working on has anything to do with that man's murder."

"That's it?"

"Not quite. We know the man who had the watch came into that shop and tried to sell what I am pretty well convinced was the Onion. The shopkeeper wouldn't pay what he wanted back then. He described the man as big, like he went for breakfast more than once. He had himself a pretty fine suit of clothes. When he came back here lately, that suit was out at the knees and the seat all shiny, like he come on hard times. We think he bought a Lee-Enfield rifle and an extra clip and that he killed the shopkeeper. Whoever is shooting at me is using an Army-issue Enfield. No one who was over there mistakes that sound."

"When did all this happen?"

"He tried to sell the watch about nineteen twenty-two or three, near as I can make it. He bought the rifle, I think, about three weeks ago."

"That don't give you much."

"No, unless we can peg it to another thing that might have happened back then."

Abel snorted. "Nothing much happened them years 'cept the Feds started enforcing the Volstead Act."

"There was a local election in twenty-four," Serena said. "I'm not sure if that means anything, but elections always make losers and winners."

"There's a thought," Jesse said. "And there is one more thing. Never mind how I come by it, a man who said he knew who killed Pa, and who got himself shot dead before he could tell me, wrote FP and the number eight on his cuff."

"F and P and a eight? What in tarnation is that all about? Somebody's initials, you think? And the number eight. Where you going with that?" Abel said. "Hey, you, Johnnie, you play nice or you're in the corner for the rest of the visit. Is this any way to carry on at your grandma's?"

"Not going anywhere yet. I suppose I could dig through the telephone book and look for names that begin with F and attached to a last name beginning with P."

"How many of them can there be?"

"Local don't always mean 'living in,' you know. Anybody living ten miles in any direction would use Floyd as their home base. That don't mean they have a local telephone. Then there is the problem of party lines and who's where."

"Thank you, Abel, for them encouraging words. No, I don't think I'll tackle the phone book just yet. That man with the Lee-Enfield is going to make a mistake and then we'll have him. Funny, he must think I know more than I do. I reckon if he'da just laid low, the chances of me flushing him out are pretty slim, especially since the sheriff don't want no part of this."

Addie heaved herself from the rocker and called the children in. "Time for pie and buttermilk. Then you all needs to be on your way whist there's still light."

● ● ● ● ●

Jesse thought they must look like gypsies heading home. Willie Kick sat in the backseat with Tommy and Jake Sutherlin. Little Jess occupied the space on the front seat between Jesse and Serena and had to watch his knees whenever Jesse shifted the gears. Lady dozed in Serena's lap. Jesse wondered if maybe he should look into buying a bigger car. He'd seen advertisements for the Ford station wagon and it looked pretty snappy. You could easily fit seven or eight folks in it. Well, you could if half of them were children.

They dropped Willie Kick off at his boardinghouse and headed home. With Kick out of the way, the children were rearranged. They were all asleep in seconds.

"You didn't say anything about the timber rights you got hold of. Was there a reason?"

"Serena, I have this feeling, you know deep down, that letting on about that right now is not a good idea. Maybe it's because if it gets around I…sorry, we…done that, the sheriff will decide that the shooter is someone looking to get them away from me. I think now is not the time to put all of our cards on the table. Also…I don't know. Something's not quite right down at the mill and I want to keep my path clear."

"Makes sense to me. Now do you want me to tell you why I aim to pull our money from the bank?"

"You can try."

"Okay. Here's how it goes. The banks loan money, right? The amount they can loan at any one time is a function of their total deposits. To figure that out they reckon on how much is coming in and how much out and that's the amount of hard cash they keep. Then they can loan money over and above. Just as long as they can transact their daily business, they can loan money willy-nilly. The amount they need to have on hand as a percentage of the whole money assets, that'd be accounts receivable—loans and such—is called the loan to asset ratio, the LTAR. Like I said, I discovered that our bank is running at about ten percent."

"Wait, you're saying the bank loans out more money than it has?"

"Way more and if, say, folks got wind of that and went to the bank to get their money, they couldn't. The banks would have to call in their loans, which means that some folks who were planning on making a profit would have to sell their shares at a loss, and so on."

"How in Holy Ned can a bank do that?

"They just do. So, for now, Jesse, to be on the safe side, I figure we'll keep our money in the strong box in our closet."

"How'd you figure all this out?"

"I read books, Jesse, I read books."

Chapter Twenty-eight

The next morning, Monday, Jesse left the house early. He had started at the mill by trying to be the first on the job and the last to leave. He thought it set an example for the men who worked the mill. Also, there wasn't a job he asked them to do that he wouldn't do himself, and at one time or another, hadn't done. Setting an example, he thought, made the work go easier. It had worked for him during his brief stint as an officer in France. Men followed leaders who showed they were as willing to share the ordeal as they were. Most days, well, until lately, until this business with the Onion started, he would be the one to unlock the gate, fire up the engines, and turn on the lights. R.G. had been understanding and Henry Sturgis had filled in, but today it was time to get back to normal. He turned onto the access road and pulled up. The gate was wide open and even at this distance and with the car motor running, he could hear the zing of saws slicing through wood. Work had begun. He drove on in and parked next to R.G.'s Cadillac and an elderly Studebaker he did not recognize.

R.G. greeted him with a wave and started to say something, but Henry Sturgis, who was sitting at the desk Jesse used when he came into the office, cut him off.

"Good morning, Jesse. I guess you haven't heard and R.G. was about to tell you. As it's my place to do the talking now, you need to know that me and R.G. has come to an agreement and I have bought this mill."

"Sorry, Jesse," R.G. said, "but I did give you the chance."

"No problem there, R.G. So, I guess congratulations are due here, Henry."

"Yep. Thank you. So, here's the thing, Jesse, with me now owning this place, there isn't any need for you to be here anymore."

"Wait, you're letting me go?"

"Well, like I said, I pretty well got the hang of this operation, so I don't need a foreman, that'd be you. Oh, and another thing. While I was back home, I married my sweetheart, Shirley MacDougal. That'd make her Shirley Sturgis now. Anyway, she's done books for her father's store, so I won't be hiring your wife, either. If you'll just kindly bring the books in, my wife will take over that job. Oh, I brought you a box so's you can clear out your stuff in this desk."

Henry took a long look around the office, smiled, and left.

"Well, I sure didn't see this coming, R.G."

"Sorry, Jesse. If I had known what he was aiming to do, I wouldn't have sold him the place. If only you had taken up the offer."

"R.G., it ain't your fault. There was no way I would have bought this mill. I am surely attached to it, you know, but Serena wouldn't have let me, even if I wanted to."

"Why is that?"

"She says there's something about your debt load that put her off."

R.G.'s face lit up with a rare grin. "What did she say?"

"Umm, well, with respect, R.G., she said that whoever bought the mill took on the debt and that practically doubled the price, so to say, and she suspected you might know that and were looking to get out from under and cash out."

"You are married to one very smart woman. You do know that, right? The day that girl walked in here ten years ago and asked for a job, I knew that. You keep her close, Jesse."

"She was right?"

"Oh, yeah. Your smarty pants friend, Henry, there, has a lot to learn. I ain't well, you know that. I depended on you to turn the profits. I looked at this operation, the way we set it up milling hardwoods for furniture, was a good strategy, but you can see it has a limit and now…well, as I said, I am not well, so, as every good bank robber would say, I aimed to take the money and run."

"You old dog, you are no more gone off the farm than me."

"I will tell you the truth, now that it can't happen, that it would have hurt my heart if you had bought this place under the circumstances."

"But you'da sold it to me anyway."

"You know what I always say, right? Business is business, Jesse. So what about Henry? It's a mean thing he did to you."

"Yeah, well, what do you expect from a man who'd shoot himself in the foot to avoid combat? Much as I hoped otherwise, Henry wasn't ever going to walk straight."

"He done that? God Almighty, I swear, I would never have sold this mill to a gol-durned coward, if I had known that. Son of a bitch!"

"Yes, you would, R.G. Business is business. Maybe not to him, but to somebody. Listen, that war wasn't no Spanish American adventure—all due respect to you and Colonel Roosevelt. It were a misery with no chance for a good outcome. Henry wasn't the only doughboy who took a quick exit, and if you count all the ones who didn't shoot themselves but surely thought about it, well…there you go."

R.G. sighed. "It's getting to be a world I don't understand anymore. So what will you do now?"

Jesse shrugged. "There's always something out there. I suspect something will turn up. Maybe I'll apply for the police. That way maybe I could get somewhere with finding out who killed my pa. Probably not. Who knows? I'll find something. We ain't broke. We'll be good for a spell. By the way, how're the orders holding up? It ain't no business of mine no more, 'course, but are things getting back to normal?"

"Nope. In fact we have some more cancellations. I told Henry, but it didn't register. He said he's got himself some promises up north from furniture folks he says he knows, and he's thinking things are going to turn. He has an appointment with the bank to set up another line of credit so he can buy more equipment. He thinks he has a backup plan."

"Which is?"

"He didn't say, but I suspect he thinks he could convert back to soft woods."

Jesse grinned. "Well, there is that, and good luck to him. I hope he has them orders from up north in writing. By the way, that smart woman you were talking about just now would tell you to get your money into something solid, not a bank deposit. She says—"

"That the banks are a risky place to put your money these days, right? She's right. Well, I did some digging, you know. I mean if you're going to take the ride into the sunset, you check out the horse you plan to ride on. There's some things, instruments the financial folks call them, that can survive most anything the economy can throw at you. Coupon bonds, preferably with utilities, but with companies and institutions that aren't never going away, things like that. I reckon I'll be alright."

"It's been a pleasure, R.G. You have yourself a great retirement."

"While it lasts, yep, I will. Good luck to you, too, Jesse."

Jesse packed the few things he wanted to take with him in the box and left the office. Henry called out to him as he opened the car door.

"Hey, don't forget to bring in the books, right?"

"Henry, I don't work here no more, so giving me an order don't carry no weight. You want them books, you hustle your backside on over to my place and pick them up your ownself.

They'll be on the front porch steps." Jesse scanned an overcast sky and shook his head. "It might could rain soon so, you should probably get to that pretty quick."

Jesse started his car and drove home. Now, how to tell Serena that both of them were out of work?

Chapter Twenty-nine

Jesse recounted what happened at the mill. He waited for Serena to react. They had never faced anything quite like this and he was unsure what she would do. She sat motionless, face like a granite statue, and eerily silent. The seconds ticked away. He began to worry. Had he put her into a state of shock? Should he get help?

"Serena…?"

She held up her hand, palm toward him.

Jesse sat back. "Well, okay, then…"

She took a deep breath, shook her head, and gave him a crooked smile. "You are a trusting and nice man. So you shouldn't be faulted for putting a snake in with the chicks. We are okay for now, Jesse. We have been careful with our money and we aren't going to starve anytime soon. We might think about moving back up the mountain, though. That'd save on rent money. Not right away, I don't mean. There's the children's schooling, but for now, you don't need to fret yourself over how we are going to get by."

"You're sure?"

"Positive. Now, you said what about the books?"

"I said if he wanted his books, he'd better come fetch them. I wasn't working for him anymore and that was that. I said they'd be on the porch steps."

"You do know it's likely to rain and they might be ruined?"

"It might have crossed my mind."

"Might have? I hope this new wife of Henry's knows about double entry bookkeeping. If she doesn't, you can expect a howl and some serious crow-eating before too long."

Serena gathered the books together, sorted the piles of invoices and bills, pulled the checkbook from the center drawer, and made a pile in the center of the rolltop desk she used as her office. She transferred the pile into an old milk crate and covered the lot with a scrap of oilcloth.

"I worked too hard on these books over all those years to see them ruined in a rainstorm. I know you'd like that, but we need to be better than him, Jesse."

Jesse knew she was right. He winked and carried the box to the steps. He paused, his eyes on the oilcloth.

"Don't you even think about it, Jess. You just put that box down and come in for coffee. We need to do some planning."

● ● ● ● ●

Sometime late that afternoon, the box on the porch steps disappeared. Neither Jesse nor Serena heard a car or person, but it did vanish. Meanwhile, Serena made a trip to the bank. She told Jesse that she had removed all but the last five hundred dollars from their account.

"All but...all but five hundred? Good God A'mighty, Serena, how much money do we have?"

"Don't you go using the Lord's name in vain in the house and around the children. We have enough."

"Well, I reckon. Five hundred left over from what?"

"Jesse, bless your heart, you are purely a money dope. I knew that two days after we were married and—"

"And that's why you are in charge of the money. I know."

"Back when you first started at the sawmill, you remember how you made a decent wage, but you also sold timber rights to R.G. and some other folks on the side?"

"Well, sure."

"A whole lot of timber rights?"

"I guess so."

"Well, I banked all that money and any leftover we might have at the end of a week. We've been living on your salary and what I bring in, or did, from the mill. We have, with interest, managed to build us a little nest egg. I was hoping to buy this house outright, but wasn't going to be the one to start the bargaining."

"Why?"

"The advantage in any confabulation is always with the person being asked. That means the one who starts the talk is the one who wants something. If he wants it badly enough he's likely to give more than he might if it was the other way around, see? I'm waiting for Lawyer Bradford to open the conversation."

"I am married to the devil's daughter."

"Glad you finally figured that out. Now maybe you'll pay me more mind."

• • ● • •

By Wednesday, the Sutherlins had settled into a new routine. Jesse spent the mornings in town sounding out various merchants and businesses about employment. He'd no success thus far, but Serena's reassurance that they had more than enough to sustain them for a long time kept him from worrying as much as he might have done. He dropped in on Nicholas Bradford on Friday. Bradford had always been a friend and supporter, and Jesse thought he ought to know what had happened. And he might also have a lead or two on where he might find work.

"Jesse, my friend, I am surely sorry to hear about your plight, I am. I will sound out my acquaintances and see what I can do. Now, it's funny you came to me just now because I was aiming to have a chat with you about an opportunity that has come my way. It is a chance to turn pennies into dollars. It is a can't-miss.

I plan to buy in big and I was hoping you'd be able to join me, but now I reckon that can't happen. So, how are you fixed for cash? I can't do much, but I might be able—"

"We are just fine, thank you. Serena has been salting away cash for a spell and we're good."

"Money in the bank?"

Jesse hesitated answering. Should he warn Bradford about that LTAR business? He reckoned a smart man like him would know and he didn't need to know that Serena had pretty much emptied their money from the bank.

"Yep, we're good. Real good, as a matter of fact, so no worries here."

"Well, I'm pleased to hear that, yes, indeed. Good to know."

Friday afternoon brought the predicted cry for help. Shirley Sturgis stood at the foot of the porch steps. Serena and Jesse stared down at her.

"See, Missus, I kept my father's books for him in his store, but it weren't like what you have here. Can you show me how this works?"

"It's simple double-entry bookkeeping, Ma'am. You kept books, you know all about that."

"Double-entry…what? No, all I did was write in the cost of what came in and the price paid on what went out and at the end of the day, just figured out if we was ahead or behind."

"I see. You didn't do any bookkeeping at all, then. I reckon the books your husband handed you must look like Greek. Well, here's what I think you should do. There are a dozen books in the library about double-entry bookkeeping. I think you should just hop on over there and get yourself educated."

"Library?"

"Yep. It's a very nice place. You'll like it."

"My husband is real anxious that he get a sense of where we are, you know, financially. I thought, I hoped, you might spare me some time to show me this afternoon. I mean, how long would it take?"

"It took me six months of hard study to get there, Sis. I can't show you anything in an afternoon. No, your husband made a quick and not-thought-through decision. He's going to have to live with it. Good-day to you."

Serena turned and went into the house. Shirley Sturgis looked like she was about to collapse.

"Mister Sutherlin, I know you probably are not happy and all about how Henry went about this, but you have a good heart, I can tell. Can't you talk to her?"

"Talk to her? She is a mountain woman, Ma'am. You don't know what that means since you come from someplace where there ain't no such a thing, but you need to know that you just don't turn a mountain woman around who's made up her mind. Short of using a howitzer, anyway. Sorry, can't help you. The library is two blocks down from the General Store. You know where that's at?"

She shook her head. Jesse thought he saw tears in her eyes and almost relented. Then he thought of the response he'd get from Serena and reckoned he'd rather feel a sense of guilt over Shirley Sturgis' predicament than face what he knew would be coming from the devil's daughter if he did.

"Ask around. Someone will set you straight."

He followed Serena into the house.

• • ● • •

"Well, what are you going to tell your ma this evening?"

Sunday and church had come off without a hitch. The children were blissfully unaware of the family's changed circumstances, although Jake did ask why his pa wasn't off to the mill anymore.

Jesse said he was exercising his options. Lady asked what options were.

"Choices, chances, and maybes," Jesse had said.

Oddly, that seemed to satisfy them.

"I guess I know better than to try to keep anything from her. I reckon I will tell her the varnished truth."

"You mean the unvarnished truth."

"Nope. I plan to polish it up a bit so it looks good enough to pass muster but not fret her. She doesn't need any more aggravation at her time of life. Anyway, Willie Kick is coming and he mostly knows what happened. Otherwise, I wouldn't say anything."

● ● **●** ● ●

Monday morning found Willie Kick sitting on the front porch.

"Willie, why ain't you down to the mill?"

"I been laid off, like you. Henry Sturgis said he didn't need a grease monkey full-time just to keep a couple of engines running, so he let me go. He did say if he had need of me, he'd call me in. Nice of him, right?"

"Henry is all heart. What else is new down there?"

"Well, he ain't said but I hear there's been more orders canceled. He's thinking about ripping soft woods for the building trade."

"Is he, now? Now, that there is interesting. Where's he expecting to come by the logs?"

"He says the hills around here are full of harvestable timber."

"They are, and guess who owns all the timber rights to them trees?"

"Who?"

"Me."

"No."

"Yep. If Henry is aiming to saw pine, he's going to have to

deal with me. Come on in and have some breakfast. I have a proposition to run by you."

"I done ate but I'll take a cup of coffee."

He settled Willie and called for Serena to join them.

"Here's the thing. I was down to the Mercantile last week, you know, just poking around, and I went around back. They used to have a lumber yard there but DeGroot let it go. Said it was more trouble than it was worth."

"You are planning on opening a lumber yard?" Serena said. She did not look convinced.

"Let me finish. So, I'm poking around back there and I see some kind of machinery under a big old tarp. I pulled it off and what do you think I found?"

"No idea. What?"

"A complete set-up to saw logs. Tracks, mandrel, dogs, the works. There was even a blade in place. It was pretty rusty and I don't reckon it would cut butter, but the rest looked to be in pretty good shape. We'll need to knock off the rust of a bunch of years but, it'll do, I think."

"You fixing to go into competition with Henry."

"I'm fixing to letting him think I am in competition with him. In fact, if we can mill out some board feet and sell them, so much the better. It could be a going concern either way. The point is he needs to understand he don't treat folks that way without consequences, see?"

"And where do I fit in?" Willie asked.

"Why, you're my partner. I figure instead of rent for the lot and equipment, we'll pay DeGroot a penny a running foot. The fellas cutting the timber, maybe two cents, and you and me will split what's left over fifty-fifty."

"A lumber yard. You and me?"

"Well, why not? Are you still in touch with the men out at the camp? If they can learn sawmilling, we can put two or three of them to work, too."

Serena gave Jesse "the look," but held her tongue.

Chapter Thirty

After talking the idea through and with Serena's less-than-enthusiastic endorsement, Jesse and Willie drove into town. They needed to strike the deal with DeGroot, the owner of the lot behind the Mercantile on which they planned their milling operation. Also, Jesse wanted to check in with the sheriff. He didn't expect to hear anything useful, but he thought if he persisted, Privette might give him some help, if only to hush him up. The mornings were turning chilly and cold air slipped through the windows and doors. Jesse wondered why someone didn't invent a heater for automobiles. With all that hot water in the radiator, you'd think some handy fella could divert it into a heat box in the front. Maybe even rig up an electric fan to push the warm air around.

"You're a handy person, Willie. Do you reckon you could rig up a pipe off of the radiator and run hot water back into a heater box in the cabin?"

"Already been done, Jesse. The new A model Fords, they say, will offer that next year, which, of course, is this year."

"No!"

"S'truth."

"I would like to get me one of them, especially that station wagon they got coming."

"Maybe you'll strike it rich and then you can. Everybody says you should get into the stock market. There's fortunes being made there every day."

"Don't believe everything you hear, Willie. You know what they say, if it sounds too good to be true, it probably is."

"Well, I will tell you this, Jesse, if I could get my mitts on a few hundred dollars, I'd not be thinking about making a living sawing yellow pine. Even I know there's nothing that fouls a saw blade quicker that sap-heavy pine."

"Well, then, that can be your next big project. Since Mister Ford put you out of the car-heater business, how about you having a think on how to keep the blade slick when we saw new-cut pine?"

"I can tell you right now, but you won't be liking it."

"How?"

"You are just spraying the blade down with gasoline. It dissolves the sap like nobody's business *und*, bingo, no binding in the blade."

"Gasoline? Are you plumb off your bean? And when she gets hot or the track sparks when we rotate the log and the whole thing goes up like a land mine?"

"I said you wouldn't like it."

They pulled up to the Mercantile and went to search for DeGroot. They found him in the closet that served as his counting room. A large safe stood in the corner with its door open. DeGroot stood at a low counter pushing coins of various denominations around with a stubby finger. He had piled them in fours and fives, except for the six silver dollars and the twenty-five-dollar gold piece. Once done he tapped each pile adding them as he went.

"So, six and one, two three—that's twelve and zen one... ummm... fourteen , tap, tap, tap twenty-six plus twenty-five to make fifty-one. Hello, Jesse. You're here to talk some business, yes?"

"Yes. This here is Willie Kick. He's going to be my partner."

"What kind of name is this, Kick?"

"What kind of a name? Well, my folks come here from Bavaria and—"

"There is no deal for the lumber yard, Jesse. Sorry. You're a nice boy and you fought in the war, but there will be no Bosche working in my yard."

"Shoot, Mister DeGroot, Hervel, the war been over for ten years."

"I am Belgian, yes? Do you not know what the Germans did to Belgium? Have you seen? They did not need to destroy whole cities. There was no resistance. They burned defenseless towns and cities. Then they shelled them anyway. Pigs, animals. Bosche."

"Look, Hervel, this here Willie. He fought for our side. He mighta been born one way, but he turned out another. Tell him, Willie."

"That a fact, Mister DeGroot, and I saw what the Germans did. After the Armistice, my unit, we walked over to there. It was bad. Some of my *kommaraden*, friends, was so angry they went looking for those men, those Germans, and the few they found they beat up pretty bad. Yes? Even me, they gave the dirty look. So, yes, I know. But you know, I am on the American side fighting."

"This is true?"

"Yes sir, it is," Jesse said. "Now Willie here is a mechanical genius and can do numbers pretty good. I'm fixing to make a call downtown. You and him can fix up a deal that works for all of us."

● ● ● ● ●

Jesse left the two men talking about the war, Belgium, and, he hoped, business. He drove to the sheriff's office. He'd just pulled into a spot across the street when he noticed Dalton Franklin coming out of the building.

Dalton P. Franklin had been a thorn in Jesse's side since he came home from France. Franklin had lost to David Privette in his attempt to stay sheriff, but still posed a problem for Jesse and some others, even now. So, was the former sheriff looking for a job, maybe? Since he lost his election, he'd had difficulty finding anyone to hire him except his cousin Willard Smith, who'd given him his old job back as night watchman at his ice houses. If Dalton hadn't been such a petty, mean-spirited and dishonest man, Jesse might have felt sorry for him.

No, actually he wouldn't have. There was too much bad blood between them to ever engender a sense of common humanity. Apparently, most of the town shared that position.

When Franklin had driven away, Jesse climbed the three steps to the office door and pushed in. Privette did not seem pleased to see him.

"You come here to turn yourself in?"

"For what?"

"Gutting Manikin, being a nuisance, anything?"

"None of them. I came to ask if you had any leads on who's been shooting at me. Also, I thought you should know that Willie Kick, who works with me, can definitely identify the man in the shop the afternoon Manikin was killed."

"He can? Who is it?"

"He don't know who. He's new to town. What I mean, if he saw him, he'd know him."

"That ain't much."

"But it's something. Look, Sheriff, I don't know what put a bee in your bonnet about me. I thought we was on pretty good terms. Be that as it may, this here is serious business. There is a crazy man out there shooting at me. Will he start in on my family next? The only reason I can think he'd be doing that is because he thinks I'm getting close to figuring out who killed my pa."

"Are you?"

"I got nothing yet, but that don't seem to stop him. I'm asking you. Is there anything you can tell me? Anything you might have turned up, heard, guessed?"

"Jesse, at the outset, I told you to keep your nose out of this. You didn't listen and now you got someone, who might or might not have anything to do with this business, shooting at you. And, no, I ain't got anything, either. Take some advice, back off. Tell folks you're done and maybe you'll live to see Christmas."

"Is that what Dalton Franklin was in here about? Whether I'd live 'til Christmas? He tried TO RAILROAD ME FOR A KILLING once. Does he really want another go?"

"You don't sit high in his dance card, Jesse, and why he was here is none of your business. Now take my advice. Let it go."

"That ain't my way, as you probably know, and since I don't work at the sawmill anymore, I got more time. Just letting you know, David. I am not done."

Chapter Thirty-one

Jesse left the sheriff's office, but not without first noticing that Dalton Franklin's car had reappeared and now sat parked across the street. There was no sign of the fat ex-sheriff, though.

He drove to Mort's Garage. If he remembered correctly, Mort had a busted-up Model T sitting in his back lot. Its front end was all smashed in, but he thought the motor and drive chain might be workable. If it was, and if he could jaw-bone a deal from Mort, he'd have his power supply to drive the saw.

Mort was agreeable to a little haggling and they made a deal. Jesse was very pleased with himself and drove back to the Mercantile. Willie had his work cut out for him. Somehow he'd have to find a way to fit a wider wheel to the back end of the T Model. The wheel that mounted a tire would be several inches too narrow to accommodate the belt that powered the saw blade.

He found Willie working his way through a stack of clean rags as he oiled and wiped the rig's track.

"I got us a power source, but it'll need some work," Jesse said as he shed his jacket and grabbed a handful of rags.

"What'd you get?"

"After Mort and I did some jawboning, the back end of a Model T. The motor runs and the wheel spins. We'll need to resurrect the radiator and modify the wheel, though."

"And just where did you jaw Mort down to?"

"If it works, we owe him ten dollars. If it don't, it's on us to get the carcass to the town dump."

"Fair enough. How're we going to get the old wreck here?"

"I reckon I'll borry me a truck somewhere."

The rifle's report, a sharp crack of a Lee-Enfield that Jesse would recognize anywhere, arrived at the instant he saw Willie spin and heard him gasp. Willie crumpled to the ground.

Jesse yanked his pistol free and snapped off four shots back along what he assumed to be the line of fire. He had no illusions about his .32 caliber pistol. He knew it did not have the range to hit anything at that distance, but he hoped if he put enough elevation on the barrel, he might lob one or two bullets into the general area. He thought he heard a thump, but couldn't be sure.

DeGroot burst through the door and stared at Willie on the ground.

"You shot this man?"

"No. Hand me some of them clean rags."

He grabbed a handful from DeGroot and packed Willie's wound.

DeGroot stood by, shuffling his feet. "But I hear shots, there you are with the gun. So, why did you—?"

Jesses tore some rags into long strips, tied them together, and cinched them around the crude dressing he'd made.

"Didn't, Mister DeGroot. Give me a hand with Willie. I have to get him to the hospital. Help me put him in the car."

DeGroot did as he'd been asked. "But, Jesse, your gun and the shooting?"

"Call the sheriff and tell him what happened. I have to get going, okay?"

He slammed the door shut, jumped into the driver's seat and tore off. Not to the local dispensary. Jesse knew a serious gunshot wound when he saw one and this one for sure wasn't the first. He headed to Christiansburg. It boasted a full-scale hospital. He'd have gone all the way to Roanoke if he thought Willie would survive the trip. Willie needed a surgeon and some real nursing if he was going to survive this, and the order of the day was to get to them as quickly as possible.

● ● ● ● ●

An attendant and a nurse helped Jesse wheel Willie into the emergency area. The attending physician shook his head and wondered how long the man would last, considering the nature of the wound. Jesse wanted to knock this young whelp silly. Instead, he asked if there was a surgeon handy and an OR.

"We got an operating room, but I'm what you get for a surgeon. I don't have an anesthetist. I'll have to send for one and I don't have an OR nurse to help me, either."

"Okay, listen. This ain't the first wound I seen like this, Doc, and I worked a few patch-ups in my time in France. If we wait for all them folks to get here, get themselves scrubbed up, and so on, Willie, here, will die." He turned and surveyed the meager staff. "How about you, Sis? You up to dropping ether for the doc?"

The nurse glanced at the attending and then at Willie. "I reckon I could try. Yes, sir."

"Okay, then, Doc, let's us scrub up in some carbolic and fix this man."

"This is beyond my authority. You have no training. The nurse is not permitted to administer anesthesia and—"

Jess let his jacket flap open. The doctor saw the gun on his hip and swallowed.

"Just so you know, Doc. I am one of them men you have heard about who lives up on Buffalo Mountain. I reckon you know what that means."

"The OR is this way."

● ● ● ● ●

As it turned out, the nurse was a more-than-capable anesthetist and Jesse quite adept as the operating room nurse. Except for scalpel, and sutures, the nomenclature of the OR was a mystery to Jesse. The doctor had to point to the various instruments he needed. When the doctor had extracted the bullet and held it out on the end of a forceps, Jesse offered a pan and smiled when it clanked in as the doc released it. That slug was going home with him.

They found Willie a room, made him comfortable, and agreed that the operation never happened. Jesse had brought him to the hospital in pretty much the state he currently was in. The nurse seemed pleased with herself. Jesse couldn't tell what was on the doctor's mind. He fished out a pint of his grandfather's best moonshine from under the backseat of his car and pressed it on the doc. They had an understanding.

The registrar was another matter. That stern woman had paperwork to complete. Two twenty-dollar bills and the assurance that he, Jesse, would be good for all further costs, persuaded her to accept the new patient. So, Bill Cook of Buffalo Mountain was admitted to the hospital, listed as having incurred a superficial wound in a hunting accident.

Jesse headed home. He needed Serena's brain working on this, but wasn't sure how he was going to tell her how they'd come to this point.

Chapter Thirty-two

Twilight faded and the kitchen slipped into semidarkness. The coffee in Jesse's cup had turned cold and the slice of apple pie remained untouched on his plate. A single candle flickered on the table. Mister Edison's electric light bulbs were fine for sweeping up, sorting clothes, but failed at providing the soft light needed for romance or, in this case, contemplation. Serena stood, removed their cups, and stepped to the back door. She flung the contents out into the night, returned, refilled them, but still remained silent.

It had taken Jesse an hour to tell her all that had happened—the shooting, the hospital, all of it. He'd had to back up two or three times, but he'd told it all. Now he waited. Serena stared unseeing at a point somewhere in the next room. Jesse shuffled his feet.

"Not yet, Jess."

He sipped at his coffee.

Lady appeared at the door in her nightie and dragging a Raggedy Ann doll. "Mama?"

"You get yourself back upstairs this minute, Lady." Serena never spoke harshly to the children. She didn't this time either, but the tone, timbre, something signaled to the little girl that this was not the night to test her mother. She turned and mounted the stairs without a word. All you might have heard was the soft thump, thump of Raggedy Ann's head on the risers.

"Where's Willie now?"

"Christiansburg Hospital, registered as Bill Cook."

"There is a why needing an answer here."

"I had to consider that Willie was the target, not me, and if so, I needed him tucked away where nobody might find him. Lying in a hospital bed would be like—"

"Shooting fish in a barrel."

"No, not that. Did you ever try to shoot fish in a barrel? Can't be done. Me and Charlie McAdoo tried it one day and we must have used up two boxes of shells. Never did get that fish."

"Jess, you're drifting."

"Sorry. Anyway, he should be safe enough. I'll move him later."

"Where?"

"My notion is to tuck him away in our place on the mountain. Amy and Ma can slip over twice a day to change his dressings and feed him. I thought I'd mention it to Big Tom and you can bet your last greenback no stranger would get within fifty yards of the house 'fore he'd be looking down the barrel of some kind of firearm."

"Hmmm. I guess that would work. So, let me get this straight, you've been shot at three times and every time the shooter misses you and hit somebody or something else: the man from the hobo camp, the car up on the mountain, and now Willie, correct? You believe the shooter is using a Lee-Enfield rifle like the one you all carried in the war and so that means he could be a veteran like you and Willie. But he misses you."

"Yes."

"What doesn't fit here, Jess?"

"What?"

"You're still here. If he is used to firing the rifle, how's he keep missing you?"

"He's a bad shot."

"Don't you go getting smart on me, now."

"Sorry. It's not simple. See, them rifles are good, really good in the way they're put together and all, but they are not fine-tuned, you could say. The Army just wanted the doughboys to shoot at a space as fast as they could. Oh, we all went to the range trying to get us a shooting badge of some sort, but in France that didn't count for much. Every company had a man or two who would be what they came to call snipers but most everybody else just fired away. So to answer, the fact he missed me don't necessarily figure into the discussion."

"Okay, then. How about this…why is somebody shooting at you?"

"Because he knows I'm looking for the man who killed Pa, which is likely himself, and he don't want me to find out who he is."

"And how close are you to finding that out?"

"Not very. Well…nowhere."

"Listen to yourself. If you are nowhere close to finding a killer, why would he draw attention to himself by shooting at you? Why not just let you fail?"

"Because…okay, I see, I think."

"Here's another thing. One, is there anyone else who would like to take a shot at you? Two, is there anyone else who might want to shoot Willie? You said you thought he might be the intended victim. He has a sketchy past. Maybe you and your search for a killer weren't the target all along. Maybe there's two shooters."

"Now, that there dog is not going to hunt, Serena, but there is one person who would take that shot. See, Willie can identify the man in the store the day Manikin was killed. If that man is the killer, and Manikin hinted that he was the one with the watch, well…"

"See how this gets bigger when you stand this thing on its head? Okay, back to someone else, besides this killer person who might have it in for you?"

"Well, except the longstanding ruckus us McAdoos have with the LeBruns, I can't think of anyone."

"How about Henry?"

"Henry Sturgis? Why would he want to shoot me?"

"Well, maybe first, to scare you off from buying the mill. Then he gets the mill and discovers what a bad bargain he got himself and maybe he thinks you and R.G. set him up, that you were part of the plan to dump the business on him. He's stuck with books he can't read and orders heading south. Plenty up on the mountain'd take a shot at you for less than that. Third, maybe he's mad cause you stole all the timber rights away."

"That's a mess of maybes."

"It is, but you can't just overlook them. Finally, why isn't Sheriff Privette helping you?"

"That is a puzzle. I thought we was on good terms and then… well he just chilled up, you could say. He did give me one piece of advice, 'though I don't know what to do with it."

"Jess, I am exhausted. Do I want to hear this?"

"Probably not. It's another rabbit hole. It might produce a bunny. Probably won't."

Serena rose, collected their cups and put them in the sink to be washed in the morning. "You planning on eating that pie?"

"Yeah, in a minute. Maybe I'll get me a glass of buttermilk to go with it."

"Good night, then."

Serena disappeared up the stairs. A moment later, the light winked out. Jesse fetched his buttermilk and went out to sit on the back porch. It had turned cold; maybe there'd be frost tonight. He shivered, ate his pie, and sipped his buttermilk.

Two things pushed at the back of his mind. Two related things. Tailors and something Manikin said about one. What was it?

He was too tired to chase those two things down, tonight anyway. He yawned and went back inside, pulling the door closed behind him. He stood for a minute looking at the bolt, and then threw it.

He had never locked his doors before. Who did? But now

he felt like someone had eyes on him all the time. There was a fancy word for that, but he couldn't remember what it was. Might maybe have thought of that before he took his pie and buttermilk out on the porch.

He hung his hat on a peg. The gold label inside the sweatband had nearly worn away. It glinted for a split second in the candlelight before Jesse pinched out the flame between his thumb and forefinger.

Chapter Thirty-three

Jesse woke early and was downstairs before Serena or the children. He had the coffee on the hob and was beating a half dozen eggs and a cup of milk into a froth before he dumped them into a pan of hot grease. The bacon had been cooked and the rashers removed and were set to cooling on a plate. He banked down the heat for the eggs. He heard Serena's calling the children into wakefulness. When he heard her steps on the stair, he poured the eggs into the bacon grease, swirled them around, and as they began to congeal, pulled the pan away from the heat.

"You are up early, Jess. Is that from a guilty conscience or did you come up with an idea?"

"Sorry, none of them. With Willie out of commission, there's nothing I can do about getting our little sawmill back behind the Mercantile going. Besides, DeGroot has convinced himself that I shot Willie, so I think maybe I'll give him a wider berth today and head away from town."

"Why'd he think such a thing?"

"He heard shots, rushed out back and I'm the only one he sees holding a gun."

"And you were holding the gun because...?"

"I tried to lob a bullet or two back at the shooter. That's what he saw and drew his own conl...whatchacallit...that's how he got the idea."

"Uhn-hunh."

"Well, it were true in a way. Not that I shot Willie but I was doing the shooting. Anyway, I thought I'd run up to Ma's and tell her to expect some company."

"Your ma?"

"Well, sort of. When Willie is moveable, I'll take him up to our place, like I said, and fix it so's her and Amy can get over there in the morning with breakfast, change his dressings, and leave behind lunch. Then they come back in the evening with dinner, do the dressings again. I'll fetch in firewood and so on, while I'm at it."

"You're not putting him in our bed." Not a question.

"No, I figured to pull one of the boys' beds into the big room next to the kitchen stove. Easier to manage. When Abel got hisself in a bad way, that's what we done."

The children tumbled down the stairs and all attempts at holding an adult conversation went by the wayside.

● ● ● ● ●

Jesse helped clear off the dishes, corral the kids, and get them off to school. They followed their ma, tallest to short, single-file. It was a sight that never ceased to bring a smile to his face. He worried about them. What if the shooter took it into his head to go after Serena or the kids? Maybe thinking to scare him off. It wasn't the country way of doing things, but for sure times they were a-changing. He grabbed his hat off the peg, collected the keys to his car, and headed up the mountain.

He stopped at his cabin first, the one he'd built on the foundation of the old springhouse for Serena after they'd married. It wasn't much, but it was snug in the winter and breezy in the summer. It had served them well during the early years of their marriage and through the births of their children. He parked and made a complete circuit around the house before entering.

No footprints in the dust. No evidence of an attempt to whisk them away. No one had disturbed the cabin since he was last there. He scooped up an armful of firewood and pushed on in.

It took him nearly an hour to arrange the furniture to his satisfaction. He made a mental note to pick up a block of ice from the New England Ice House when he moved Willie. He took one more look around and left to tackle his mother about what he wanted her and Amy to do.

● ● ● ● ●

"You want me and the girl to do what for who? What are you playing at, Jesse? How come he can't just stay in the hospital and get hisself fixed up like normal folk? You ain't making no sense."

"Slow down, Ma. You'll work yourself into a conniption fit. You know Willie. He wouldn't hurt a fly, but he might have seen something or somebody who could be hooked up with Pa's killer. Because of that, he mighta been the target, not me."

"Well there's a ray of sunshine on a dark day. He mighta been the target, not you?"

"Listen. I don't know. Things is getting complicated. Anyway, I can't protect him in a hospital bed. Lying there, he's a sitting duck. But up here on the mountain, especially after I drop a buzz in Big Tom's ear, he'll be as safe as gold in Fort Knox."

"You expect your grandpa to stand for him too?"

"Naw, you know better'n that. He just has to put out the word and no outlander will get close to Willie. Look, all you two has got to do is fetch him a little breakfast, change his dressings, and then do it again at night."

Addie started to say something about being imposed on when she saw the sparkle in Amy's eyes. She sighed. "Violet McAdoo," she muttered. "Okay, then, Jesse, but I'm telling you straight up, I don't like bringing trouble home. We got enough already here."

"What?"

"Did you think what could happen if one of the LeBruns get a-hold of this and want to stir up some old mess?"

"We just need to make sure they don't and besides, soon's he's up and running, Willie will be long gone."

"Get on with you, now. Me and Amy will take care of your friend, Jesse. Hrumph!"

"Ma?"

"I told you before about that hat."

"Yes, Ma'am, you did." Jesse resettled the fedora more firmly on his head.

Chapter Thirty-four

The rest of the week passed slowly. Jesse kept out of sight. Things seemed quiet enough, but at the same time he knew that there was a person out there who had him in his crosshairs. He didn't want to stir up any more trouble, Lord knew, but he had to shake the tree a little. Were things quiet because the word was out that he was no closer to solving his pa's murder than ever? If so, where did that notion start?

The obvious place to start would be the sheriff's office. Privette was a known blabber-mouth. He would jaw with anybody about anything, anytime. Folks knew as he made his way from home to office, at each stop, he would fill whoever was within earshot, the news of the day. Why anyone bothered to buy a newspaper was a mystery. So, from the diner and his usual breakfast of eggs over and grits, to Mort's where he gassed up his cruiser, and on through town, the news got spread. If Privette thought the search for Jesse's pa's killer was dead in the water, so did the rest of the town. It might be time to shift the story a tad. Jesse drove to town.

●　●　●　●　●

Sheriff Privette did not acknowledge Jesse's presence. Jesse cleared his throat and shuffled his feet. Still no response.

"Okay, Sheriff, you made your point. You don't want anything to do with me. You would like to believe I shot Willie Kick, that I killed Manikin, and maybe am hooked up with Sacco and Vanzetti. I don't know what has turned your head and, by damn, I don't care anymore. You are a poor excuse for a lawman and it's a wonder the town hasn't turned into some Wild West shoot-'em-up. That said, you still have an open murder investigation on your pad and I am the only person willing to do anything about it."

"Now, you just wait a minute there, son."

"I am done waiting. I been shot at. My friend, too, and now he's dead."

"Willie Kick is dead?"

"Yes, sir, he is, and we have had how many bodies turn up since this all came to light? In all this, you ain't done nothing. So, what do you expect? You do know there is an election coming. Dalton P. Franklin says he's running again."

"That fat boob. No worries there."

"And then there is the other candidate."

"Other? Who?"

"How about me?"

"You?"

"It's a thought."

Jesse turned on his heel and left. If saying he might stand for sheriff didn't stir things up, nothing else would. He drove to Christiansburg to check on Willie. It might be time to move him to the mountain.

* * * * *

The doctor who'd helped with the surgery the week before was still in residence. The hospital did seem busier, which meant

Jesse had to be careful. What he wanted from the doc might be, well, certainly bordered on the illegal. He'd brought two quarts of Big Tom's best as his persuader.

"Doc, I have a favor to ask."

"You don't have another half-dead friend in the backseat of your car, do you?"

"Nope, not this time. Fact is, I want to relieve you of the last one I brought."

"You want to move him? Why does that require a favor from me?"

"Well, sir, it's like this. He'd be a lot safer if everybody thought he was dead. I'm thinking you'd just need to make a note on his chart or whatever it is you use to keep track of the patients, that he died and his family has removed the remains."

Jesse placed one of the quart bottles on the doctor's desk. The doc eyed it. "Is that the same—?"

"The very."

"It's against the law to declare a person dead who isn't."

"That is for sure a fact, but here's the good part. That fella in the bed ain't Bill Cook. There may be a Bill Cook somewhere in the Commonwealth of Virginia, but this ain't him. So, declaring him dead is not a problem, right?"

Jesse placed the second quart on the desk. "You'd only be saying that this person who doesn't exist…don't exist."

The doctor unscrewed the cap from the mason jar and took a sizable swig. "So, Bill Cook, who is lying in my ward, isn't real and you want me to make that official by declaring him dead. Is the about the size of it?"

"Pretty much, yep."

The doctor took another swig, shook his head. "Boy, howdy, that is some smooth liquor. You all cook this up where you come from?"

"We do."

"Okay, let's do this. If he's gone, I don't have an operation not on the books to explain and that solves another problem for me. The president of the hospital board is due here on Monday. Be good to have this all tidied up."

"There you go. One good deed deserves another."

Between them they managed to wheel Willie out on a cart, covered with a pile of laundry.

The doc gave him a shot of morphine. "That ought to hold him for a few hours. After that it's on your head."

"You got it. Bill Cook is dead and gone. Thanks."

Jesse drove off. It would be a bumpy ride to and then up the mountain. He hoped the morphine would last.

• ● ● ● •

The last few miles were the roughest. Willie came around and groaned at every pot hole and bump in the road the old Piedmont hit.

Jesse got him settled in bed, lit a fire, and told him to rest, that he'd be right back with help and then he'd explain everything. Ten minutes later he returned with Amy and Addie.

"These here folks is going to be your nurses for a while, Willie. As far as anybody knows, you are either in a hospital somewhere or dead. Either way, you're safe up here on the mountain. You heal up and when you're ready, we're gonna go after the man who put you here."

Willie closed his eyes and drifted off. Amy pulled a chair up to the bedside and sat. "Miss Addie, iff'n it's all the same with you, I think I'd like to sit a spell with Willie. You know, just in case he needs me to fetch him something or another."

"You do that, child. I'm headed back to the cabin, but you know where to find me if you need me."

Jesse and Addie left the two and stood on the porch.

"She gonna be up to this?"

"She'll more likely kill him with kindness than bad medicine. You git on home, me and Amy has got this."

She eyed his hat but didn't say anything. Jesse reckoned it a small mercy.

She went back inside and he climbed into the car, reaching up to resettle the hat a little more firmly upon his head. He paused with his hand on the brim.

The hat was a trilby and—Ma wasn't wrong—maybe somewhat the worse for wear and not for no cause. It had been eight, nine years earlier when a pedlar parked in front of the Floyd courthouse sold it to him out of the backseat of his car. The pedlar had wanted two dollars and ended up taking eighty-eight cents, which had seemed like a good deal to Jesse but might maybe have seemed like a better deal to the pedlar, seeing as how he'd got every last cent Jesse'd had in his pockets.

He pulled the hat from his head and looked inside. The gold thread on the label was near worn off but there was still enough of it there to read the name.

Samuel Schwartz.

He dropped the hat next to him and stared out the window at nothing in particular. Samuel Schwartz, haberdasher and tailor, who'd driven a car full of goods into southwestern Virginia looking for a storefront in a town in need of his services. Floyd already had a haberdasher and Jesse had recommended Picketsville.

He knocked the hat off the seat reaching for it and had to lean forward to pick it up from the passenger well by the back brim. He saw the label upside down and everything all of a sudden turned right side up.

●　●　●　●　●

Someday, Jesse thought, they will connect up all these winding roads into one nice straight one and a body could make his way up and down the Valley without having to pack a lunch. Picketsville wasn't all that far as the crow flies, but getting there took patience and a good map.

He found Sam Schwartz's shop with no problem. Sam had rented space off the lobby of the town's only hotel. It had entrances to it from both the lobby and the street.

A little bell attached to the frame tinkled as he pushed open the street door.

Chapter Thirty-five

Back in Floyd, Jesse parked a block away from the sheriff's office. From that vantage point, he could see who entered and who exited the building with the certain assurance that he would not be observed. By now the news about Willie would have made it into the rumor mill that drives most small towns. He hoped this would work. Well, Serena had said, "Stand it on its head." He had, and now he had a bead on his killer.

The problem was did he have enough to flush him out? "Circumstantial evidence," Lawyer Bradford had said, "with a sharp prosecutor, can end in a conviction, but there's nothing like a confession to put a spade in the shingle, so to speak, particularly if the scoundrel has a good defense attorney, like me." Jesse didn't know if he had enough, but he knew Bradford would not defend the killer either way. With a little bit of luck, and some fast talking, he reckoned he'd put this man over a barrel one way or another.

He saw the car pull up and park and its driver heave his bulk out and huff his way to the sheriff's office. Time to get this circus wagon moving. Jesse gathered his papers, patted the bulge on his hip, climbed out of the old Piedmont, and headed to the sheriff's office his own self.

Privette was seated at his desk, leaning forward, all ears to what his visitor was earnestly saying.

"I have it," Jesse strode in and announced. "I found the Onion, like I said I would."

"You found it? You found what? You mean that old watch?"

"The very same." Jesse pulled the watch free from his pocket and dangled it by its chain. "This is the Onion. You say something, Dalton?"

Dalton P. Franklin was looking at the Onion, hanging from Jesse's hand. He didn't answer. Jesse turned back to the sheriff, who was squinting at the watch. "How can you be so sure that's the watch you say it is?"

"It's got engraving on the inside and the Jefferson Davis medal on the end, also with a set of initials. This is the Onion, all right."

"Well, congratulations on that. So now what?"

"Ain't you going to ask me how I come by it?"

"I'll bite. How'd you come by it?"

"I reckon I owe it all to you."

"Me?"

Jesse turned to the other man in the room. "I'm glad you're here, Dalton. You applying to get your old job back? No? Well, anyway, you will want to hear this."

He turned back to the sheriff. "Yes, you, David. You said there weren't no genuine tailors in town eight years ago. That meant that whoever made his new suit must have been run up for him out of town. You see how that works?"

"Okay. And then?"

"And then I went poking around nearby towns and found a tailor who, wouldn't you know, had a client who wanted to pay for his new suit with a watch to make up the difference in what he had in cash money. See, this tailor didn't really want the watch, but he said the man was a mite intimidating, his word, intimidating, and he felt like he had to agree under the circumstances. Manikin said the man who tried to sell him a watch like the Onion was a big man and pushy, like he thought he was important or in charge.

"So now we got us the man in Manikin's shop trying to sell a watch like the Onion now in the tailor's shop trying to trade the Onion for a bespoke suit. The tailor says this is a big man who, now here's the funny part, wanted some extra batting in the lining around the left upper vest pocket. Now ain't that odd?"

"Where are you going with this, Jesse?"

"Well, I got to wondering about that and what extra batting might help do."

"What?"

"Sorry, I'm getting ahead of myself here. See, back when all this began, I ran across a group of fellas out in the woods. One of them, name of Elroy, said he had some information for me which he would sell for five dollars. He said he had known Brownie—you remember, the man with the glass eye who came to tell Ma that Pa had died of the influenza?—and he, Elroy, that is, could tell me who it was killed my pa. Well, before Elroy could tell me who it was, some summbitch with a Lee-Enfield rifle shot him down dead."

"Wait, there is a dead man I don't know about?"

"Oh, you know about him. You found his body out by the old ice house a week or so ago. That weren't where he got shot, by the way, but that story will have to wait for another day. Anyway, Elroy had something he wrote on his sleeve. It was almighty smudged but it looked like FP and a number. Those initials didn't get me anywhere. Then I twisted it around and look here, it's now DPF, which until I saw something else upside down, I didn't realize I was reading it backwards. Not two letters and a number, but three letters, and not FPD but DPF." Jesse turned to look at the former sheriff. "Now ain't that interesting, Dalton P. Franklin?"

"Sheriff, this man is a known killer and troublemaker, like I been telling you. He done in the kraut bastard, Kick, didn't he? It's your duty—"

"You hush up there, Dalton." It looked like Privette had found his spine at last. "So, what did that lead you to next, Jesse?"

"Well, I thought about it for a spell and then went to the *Floyd Reporter* and asked if maybe they had a picture of this fella." Jesse pulled the photo from his pocket and slid it across to Privette.

The sheriff drew in a breath.

"And then there is the extra batting on the pocket of that suit. What might that be for?"

"Well, what?"

"How about a badge?"

"A badge?"

"That'd be a maybe. And then there is the ice house. Who dumps a body in an ice house? Well, if the killer happened to work at an ice house…"

Jesse let that last statement sit there, and then, when it didn't seem that Sheriff Privette was going to remember it on his own, said to Dalton P. Franklin, "Say, Dalton, didn't you used to work at Smith's ice house before you went to deputying?"

Franklin didn't answer.

"Then things got moving. So I took that picture up to Picketsville and showed it to the tailor who made that suit and, 'Yep,' he said, 'that's the man." He wrote out a statement and said he's ready to testify in court." Jesse handed Sam Schwartz's statement to Privette.

"Then I took the picture up the mountain where I have Willie stashed away and showed it to him. He said, yep, this is the man he saw in Manikin's store the day Manikin was gutted with a bayonet."

Dalton P. Franklin sat up straight, hands gripping the arms of his chair. Jesse carefully didn't look at him but the sheriff did.

"Oh, yeah," Jesse said, "Willie ain't dead, and I didn't shoot him, as he will gladly tell you. He will recover. He'll have a bum arm, but he'll live. That's good news, right?"

"He ain't dead?" the sheriff said. "But you said…he ain't dead?"

"Nope. I lied about that, as it seemed like someone was pretty set on getting him dead and the only way to steer them off was to put out the word that the job was done. And here's one more thing. Remember Elroy's friend Brownie with the glass eye? The one I figure brought Ma the news about Pa dying?"

"You ain't going to tell me you found him, too."

"Yes and no. His name was Brownie. He's dead. Fell on a pitchfork up north somewhere, but here's the thing. Don't you reckon that if I asked around if anybody had seen this man," Jesse tapped the photo, "hanging round with a fella with a glass eye ten years ago, that somebody would remember it? It's not easy to forget a man with a glass eye. Abel remembered him, sure."

Dalton P. Franklin stirred more uneasily in his chair. "Look here, Sheriff, I think—"

"In a minute, Dalton," Jesse said. "Now when I laid all this out for him, my lawyer, Nicholas Bradford, says this is all circumstantial evidence, but he said a sharp prosecutor could get this fella fitted up for a noose pretty quick. Oh, and he already talked to Judge Watkins, who said he'd be happy as a pig in slop if Bradford sat in the prosecutor's chair."

Jesse finally turned and looked at the former sheriff. "You'll remember Judge Watkins, Dalton. You know, from the last time you and me was up before him. And I reckon you'll remember how that went, too. You know, I wasn't inclined to make too much of a fuss when you was thumping on me back then, as I reckoned you was sore about Bessie. But that wasn't it at all, was it? I'd come home from the war and you was afraid I'd start poking around into Pa's death. Well, you was right, you was just a little ahead of yourself, and me, too." He picked up the photograph and showed it to Dalton. "Say, this is a pretty good picture of you, don't you think?"

Privette stood and stepped toward Dalton Franklin. "Dalton, I'm going to have to—"

Franklin leapt to his feet. "He's a liar, Sheriff. Do your duty."

Jesse also stood. "I'm about ready to come over there and separate your fat head from the rest of you."

Privette turned and held out his hand to caution Jesse. In that instant, Franklin reached out and yanked Privette's police special from its holster.

"You both git over there against the wall, you hear? There ain't no way I'm going to jail. You know what them jailbirds will do to a ex-cop. No sir, not me. Damn you to hell, Jesse Sutherlin. Stand still. Okay, let me think. Okay, the way I see this going down is Sutherlin here grabbed your gun, Sheriff, and shot you and I managed to take it away and shoot him. Hell, I might get myself elected sheriff again for that."

He swung the pistol back and forth in a slow arc between the two men. As it shifted toward Privette, Jesse had his thirty-two automatic off his hip and the clip emptied in Dalton P Franklin.

The former sheriff crashed to the floor. The pistol in his hand skittered across the floor and ended at Privette's right foot.

"Jumping Jehoshaphat, Jesse, where'd you learn to do that?

"I been shot at by better men than him, Sheriff.

"Well, I reckon that ties this one up. Shoot, if he'd had just shut the hell up, he mighta got off on the circumstantial evidence business."

"Probably not going to matter. He's gut shot and the way he lived his life, I don't see him living long enough to go to trial."

Jesse picked up his hat which had fallen off his head in the scuffle and poked the crown back into shape. "It's a fine hat, this hat." He pulled it on and tugged at the brim. "A little blocking and it will be good as new."

Chapter Thirty-six
June 1929

Miss Primrose's wisp of a smile was all the greeting they were going to get from that formidable lady. She ushered Serena and Jesse into Nicholas Bradford's office and shut the door behind them. She might as well have not been there at all.

"Good news for you two," Bradford said and half stood and then sat back.

"How's that, Mister Bradford?"

"Well, not all good, I suspect. Depends on your point of view. R.G. Anderson has up and died. I don't know if you knew that."

"I heard something, but no details."

"Well, here's the thing about that. He took the money he got for the sale of the sawmill, a tidy sum, I hear, and moved to Spartanburg, South Carolina. He rented a room in a boarding-house down there and went looking for a broker to handle all his new money."

"South Carolina? Why in tarnation did he go all the way down there?"

"Next to Teddy Roosevelt," Serena said, "he had a fondness for the Old South…lost honor, all that. South Carolina was the state that set the Civil War in place, so I guess he just wanted to get closer to history."

"Maybe. Anyway he hooked up with this agent for Fenner & Beane." Bradford shuffled through the papers in a file on his desk. "Local yokel named J.B. Ramsay who, instead of putting him in the market where he could have doubled his money in eight to ten months, told him the market couldn't sustain the growth it had made and he should invest in safe securities."

"That's interesting, Mister Bradford, but I don't see where this goes to us. We got four young'uns driving Amy Cates... Sutherlin...crazy back to the house."

"Right. Sorry. I got sidetracked. The news is, he made me the executor of his will and he has named you as his heir, Jesse."

"His what?"

Serena turned to Jesse. "You get his money, Jess."

"I do?"

"You do. He thought the world of you, Jesse. You, too, Serena, so congratulations. You are now a man of means." Bradford leaned back in his chair and beamed.

"Means? What does 'means' mean?"

"Well, you ain't no Rockefeller or Vanderbilt, but you're comfortable."

"Holy Ned. So, what are we talking about?"

"There's an accounting in this here file. I haven't really looked into it all, but it appears you own a fistful of what they're calling blue chips, some municipal bonds, some big utilities, and a passel of treasury notes. Oh, and there is a certified check for the proceeds of his bank account pinned to the front."

Bradford slid the file across the desk and Serena corralled it. She slipped the banker's pin loose and inspected the check. "Twenty-one hundred dollars and seventy cents. Mercy."

"So, here's what I'm thinking, Jesse, Serena. I am in on a sure-fire investment in some mining stock out west. Copper, more'n you can imagine, just lying on the ground waiting for someone to come along and pick it up out there in Arizona. Two thousand dollars is the buy-in. You have the cash. You need to jump on this."

"Are you?"

"Um, well, that's the problem. I am spread so thin with margin buys and such, and they won't pay out for another month or two, I'm a little skint just now. I was thinking you could float me a loan for—"

"You're broke?"

"No, just have all my ready assets tied up in the market. So, like I said, if—"

Serena placed the cashier's check on the corner of Bradford's desk where he could see it. She smoothed it flat and caught the lawyer's eye.

"I reckon I have a better idea. You see this check, Mister Bradford? Well, I'm thinking Jesse will just endorse it over to you—"

"Well, that's mighty nice and—"

"Excuse me, but I'm not finished. He will endorse it over to you when you sign over the deed to the house and land we been renting from you this past year and a half."

"You want to buy that house and grounds for a paltry twenty-one hundred dollars?"

"And seventy cents, yes, sir, I do. It's not a bad deal, Mister Bradford. I know it was a Sears and Roebuck catalog house. I looked it up. It's what they called the Gladstone and it sold to whoever bought it for near to two thousand dollars FOB. Then there was the cost of the basement and foundation, then the well, and septic. I know all that. I also know that you bought the house at a foreclosure auction for a tenth of what it was worth. I figure twenty-one hundred dollars and seventy cents is a good return on your investment."

"Where'd you find this witch, Jesse? Missus, how do you know all this?"

"I'm just a poor little mountain girl that someone made a mistake of teaching how to read. You'd be surprised what you can learn in the library and the courthouse. I guess I'm like that yokel down there in Spartanburg. We don't believe everything folks say just because they claim to know something."

"Lord spare us and now you all got the vote. Miss Primrose!" The office door flew open and that woman scurried in. "Get me the deed to the Sutherlin rental and draw up a bill of sale."

● ● ● ● ●

Jesse and Serena sat in the front seat of the car staring straight ahead.

"What just happened?" he said.

"We own our house and have more money than I was likely to see in a lifetime. Did you look at the deed?"

Jesse skimmed the papers. "Whoa. We have five acres, and it says the grounds include the lot next door. The lot next door, Serena."

"Make a fine garden. Be able to grow our own food when times get hard, and they is surely going to get hard."

"Lord, I just hope I don't have to buy a pitchfork."

"What's that?"

"Never mind. How much money is there in that folder?"

Serena let her fingers walk through the edges of stock certificates, bonds, and notes. "This isn't just the money from the sale of the mill. R.G. had been saving for years and with no family, it sort of piled up. I can't say for sure how much, but it is either a big number with four zeros after it or a small number with five."

"Woof!"

"What do you want to do?"

"I'm leaving that money in your hands. Me, I just want to stay busy. Oh, and maybe get us one of those newfangled A Model Ford station wagons. We need something all of us can fit into."

She turned to him and gave him a kiss on the cheek. "You are the goodest man I know, Jesse Sutherlin. You go get yourself that Ford machine and then I think you need to go to Picketsville and visit Mister Sam Schwartz and have him make you a nice Sunday suit.

"Oh, and get a new hat. That one he sold you nine years ago has had it."

Death Is Nothing At All

Death is nothing at all.
It does not count.
I have only slipped away into the next room.
Nothing has happened.

Everything remains exactly as it was.
I am I, and you are you,
and the old life that we lived so fondly together
is untouched, unchanged.
Whatever we were to each other, that we are still.

Call me by the old familiar name.
Speak of me in the easy way which you always used.
Put no difference into your tone.
Wear no forced air of solemnity or sorrow.

Laugh as we always laughed at the little jokes that
we enjoyed together.
Play, smile, think of me, pray for me.
Let my name be ever the household word that it always was.
Let it be spoken without an effort, without the ghost
of a shadow upon it.

Life means all that it ever meant.
It is the same as it ever was.
There is absolute and unbroken continuity.
What is this death but a negligible accident?

Why should I be out of mind because I am out of sight?
I am but waiting for you, for an interval,
somewhere very near,
just round the corner.

All is well.
Nothing is hurt; nothing is lost.
One brief moment and all will be as it was before.
How we shall laugh at the trouble of parting
when we meet again!

—Henry Scott-Holland (1910)

To see more Poisoned Pen Press titles:

Visit our website:
poisonedpenpress.com
Request a digital catalog:
info@poisonedpenpress.com